W9-CHV-849

CONTENTS

Life Resources
18 Hurst Rise Road
Oxford OX2 9HQ
www.Life-Resources.co.uk

CONTENTS

Zak

Bridget Belgrave

LIFE RESOURCES

First published in 2003 by Life Resources

5 W⸻ ⸻ ⸻ OX2 7QQ

⸻ uk

Life Resources
18 Hurst Rise Road
Oxford OX2 9HQ
www.Life-Resources.co.uk

ISBN 0 953 9563 3 4

Printed and bound by Biddles Ltd
www.biddles.co.uk

This book is printed on elemental chlorine
free paper from sustainably managed forests

What people say about Ζακ

This book is really magical and amazing! Zak is a bit like me except I don't have magical powers. I wish I did. It was really interesting how he could talk to the animals and what they talked about.
Ziya, age 8

I like Zak. I could identify with him and accept him. He's not too young for me, because of the humour.
Max, age 11

I think Zak was the best book I have ever read even better than Harry Potter. I thought some bits were very funny like his first day at school.
Marion, age 9

A kind story, and highly entertaining, Zak beautifully conveys the wisdom and ways of respect, acceptance, warmth and humility. I will read it again and again.
Professor Hilton Davis, author of 'Counselling Children with Chronic Medical Conditions'

Zak is an introduction to a whole new way of life, of cultivating awareness and perceptions and tapping in to the powerful, creative inner self. It's listening to silence with pleasure, and feeling empathy non-verbally. It encourages children to feel things for themselves and to be aware of their own inner potentials, regardless of the assumptions and put-downs of others. It is a wholly healing book.
Margaret Harrison, author of 'Angels on Roller Skates'

Zak is the only novel that my son Ben, age 9, has read six times.
Anne Turner

I was delighted with Zak. He makes magic very real and ordinary. He gives it being and makes it come alive. He brings hope to find that magic in my own life.
Fr. Chris Rajendrum

Give children the precious gifts of freedom of mind and encouragement for their individuality, by exposing them to Bridget Belgrave's inspiring Zak.
Michael J. Gelb, author of "How to Think like Leonardo da Vinci"

Zak conveys simply yet profoundly the inter-dependance of the plant, animal, human and spiritual worlds.
Allegra Wint

As a Buddhist, I related to Zak very well. The 'zing' episode seemed very much like meditation and put me in mind of the woods around a few meditation centres I have been to. It was also a delight to read a book that didn't have a violent climax. My 8 year old son was fascinated by it, wondering what would happen next and often wouldn't let me finish of an evening, demanding another chapter.
Daren DeWitt

When I was a boy I was like Zak in many ways but I learnt to 'play the game'. It has only been in recent years that I got tired of the game and started trusting myself again.
Henry, who describes himself as 'a business man in seach of his soul'

This book will be welcomed by ecologists. It opens the reader's eyes to the importance of wildlife and of nature's subtle processes that can so easily be damaged - at a cost we can hardly dare to think about.
Michael Simmonds

I have just finished reading Zak. It is wonderful. He is wonderful. It is easy and fun to read and I felt as if I were inside Zak's mind a lot of the time. The message in this book really needs to be heard by millions of people. It makes me want to be Zak too!
Jane Duncan, author of 'Choose Your Thoughts, Change Your Life'

Bridget Belgrave has earned her living in diverse ways, from teaching juggling to leading workshops in nonviolent communication. She lives in Oxford. Zak is her first fiction book.

Acknowledgements

I feel grateful to Jane Corbett for leading me further into writing than I would have gone on my own; to Stella Schlag for her deep listening and her ability to bring the spirit of Zak alive in the beauty of her illustrations; to Leo Sofer for meeting Stella so I could find her and for backing us up with scans and plans; to Julia Molden and Joanna Usherwood for collaborating so patiently, flexibly and creatively to make the inside and outside of this book look how it does; to Elinor Bagenal for her warmth and her invaluable practical suggestions. I thank all at Biddles for so positively sharing their expertise in everything to do with printing. I feel touched by my friends Darby, Stephen, Miranda, Sue, Gina, Wren, Lucia, Michael & Liz who have stood by with encouragement and support all the way. And Henry, appearing out of nowhere, intuitive mystery supporter, thank you!

To my son Manuch
and my mother Susan
who showed me about childhood
freedom and thinking for yourself

CHAPTER 1

Being Unusual

Hi. My name is Zak, I'm 11, and I'm on River Island with my Mum, my brother Billy who is fourteen and a bit of a pain, and my little sister Anna. She's seven. I do have a Dad - people here sometimes think I don't, because he is working far away from here, taking people on trips on his old fashioned sailing ship around the Cyclades islands of the Mediterranean sea. He's Greek. You'd like him. He's a great guy.

The only other people on this island are the Rosens: Sam (age 12), Leah (age 8) and their Mum. They are renting the other part of the big house for the summer.

This is going to be the story of the strange and amazing summer I just spent on this island. I don't know if you have ever spent a summer on an island, but believe me, some pretty weird things can happen.

I'm actually sitting on the island right now, well, not now for you, but now for me. By the time you are reading this, I won't be here. I'll probably be back in London where I usually live. But then maybe you'll read this in a hundred years and I won't even be alive! That's strange. That's time travel.

Although I mostly want to tell you about this summer, I'm going to start with my earlier life, so you can understand a few things about me.

You see, I am not exactly a usual boy. And I started being unusual even before I was born.

Maybe you are unusual too. I used to think I was the only one, but I'm beginning to suspect there are a lot more of us than I ever imagined.

CHAPTER 2

Looking Out From Inside
age: *minus a few months*

Apparently not everyone can see out of their Mum's tummy while they are still inside, getting ready to be born.

Nobody pointed this out to me, so I took it for granted, and kept on looking.

My Mum spent a lot of time reading when she was pregnant with me. She used to sit sideways on the sofa with her feet up, and then rest the book on her extra large tummy. Well in that tummy was me, remember. She was reading Teach Yourself Plumbing. So there I was all curled up in there staring straight out at diagrams of pipe cutters and blow torches, for hours on end.

I recognised some of the things in the book.

The bath taps, for instance. They were just about at my eye level, and she went to the bathroom often enough for me to get pretty familiar with them. In fact she even collected together the tools they had in the book, and took the taps apart and put them back together again. Maybe that's what got me curious, or maybe it was the hours spent with the books right in front of my nose, but anyway, one way or another, I learned to read.

This made my life much more entertaining. I mean when she was up and about it was pretty entertaining anyway. Just going down the street to the supermarket there were all kinds of people, buses, shop windows, motorbikes, dogs. I admit the big dogs did frighten me at first. Their sharp looking teeth were altogether too close to my nose for my liking, but gradually I realised that although I could see them, they couldn't see me. This was most comforting.

Just to finish telling you about the reading though. I discovered after I'd been born, that I'd learned to read upside down. Well, you would call it upside down. It seemed fine to me, and it still does. Why not hold the book the other way up, start reading at the bottom of the page and work your way up to the top? You should try it sometime.

Later I realised why this was. I'd been stuck in one position - with my head down and my feet up - for several weeks before I was born. Up to then I could move freely, kind of like swimming. But one day I was startled to notice there was less space around me. To move involved pushing and shoving instead of easy swimming. I was stuck. The days of carefree somersaults were over. However hard I tried, I couldn't even turn over.

So from then on, whenever Mum plonked a book on me, I was looking at it upside down. I bet even you would learn to read the other way up under those circumstances.

CHAPTER 3

Getting Born
age 0

Being born was like, well, like being squeezed out of a toothpaste tube, very hard, very suddenly.

I had noticed things were getting extra tight in there for the last few days, ever since I had suddenly dropped lower down in Mum's tummy. I knew I was lower because it was a lot harder to see the words on the books she was reading and I was face to face with a new section on my Dad's trouser zip whenever he hugged my Mum, (which was pretty often, by the way).

Anyway, there I was inside her, thinking that this tightness was getting beyond a joke, and I wasn't willing to put up with it much longer, when something burst and I felt like a hovercraft come in to land - suddenly in contact with a lot of hard and bony surfaces. Then the squeezing started. This was too much. I'm getting out of here, I thought, and fast. I began to squirm, as best I could. My legs were all bent up against me, so this wasn't easy, but I could just get my toes onto some sort of bony ridge, so I pushed as hard as I could on that and I felt my head move forward a little. I could tell this was going to be hard work. It was the hardest thing I had had to do so far. OK, learning to read hadn't been easy, but I had been able to take my time over it.

I could hear my Dad flapping. He was pretending not to be worried, but I don't know why he bothered as it was obvious that he was dead scared. This didn't exactly reassure me. My Mum herself wasn't saying much. She had gone quiet, except for her breathing which sounded like someone had got out the bellows.

I gave another shove and heard my Mum gasp with pain. This shocked me. I hadn't meant to hurt her. How was I going to get out of here then, without hurting her? It was time to do some quick thinking.

It's not easy to think when you are being crushed on all sides, like Indiana Jones in the Temple of Doom. My Mum had watched this movie just last week, and I had had quite a good view. How was it Indiana had escaped?

I couldn't see much, I could hardly move, and there weren't any knobs or levers. I'd have to use my mind. I thought of the dreams I'd had about flying. It was such a nice sensation - just light and slow and streaming forwards gently through the air. I didn't seem to be a fast flyer in my dreams, or to fly high - I was always just a few feet off the ground and horizontal. I thought of that nice steady, easy, streamlined way of moving forwards. The harder I felt squeezed, the harder I thought of flying, and then my ears popped, and the lights came on, and I was really out there, flying across the room, nice and slow, heading for the door.

What a surprise the colours were. It had never occurred to me that things would look different when I came out. It was so much clearer and brighter, and the colours were astonishing, pink and yellow and blue. The bedspread looked positively alive. And the sounds. All separate and crisp as if the bath had stopped running.

Suddenly I heard a sound I was sure I had never heard before, not even in muffled form. This was volume gone crazy. I didn't know anything this loud existed. It was a scream. A double scream. It was my Mum and Dad screaming simultaneously. I didn't know they were capable of it. They really should join the opera.

Their ear splitting scream broke my concentration and I crashed to the ground. As I know only too well now, I can only fly when I concentrate. Luckily I wasn't seriously hurt. Probably because I landed on the bed. This was the first sign that I am a lucky person.

CHAPTER 4

Finally I Can Talk
age 1

Generally, I did the normal baby things when I was a baby. For instance, I lay around experimenting with moving my small, pudgy body. It was disappointing not to be able to move more easily. I'd loved swimming around inside my Mum, before I ran out of space that is. It seemed a cruel joke to emerge into this bigger than ever space and find myself beached on the bouncy baby chair.

So I set to work moving whatever part of my body I could. At first it was hard work just to get my arms to flap while I lay on my back. Gradually I got my legs going, and after what seemed like months of effort I managed to organize myself to crawl. I could see there were better things to come just from looking around at the people standing and walking. It's funny, when I was inside my Mum I never realised that all those people had actually learned to stand upright and walk. I kept trying, but every time I crashed over. I'd have to settle for crawling for a while. Anyway, it was a relief to be able to scoot about somehow.

This was when I started my serious research. How did everything feel - those little holes where the plug went in to the wall, the rice as it poured out of it's packet, the cat's tail?

Sometimes my research got me into trouble. Like the time I tested the balance of Billy's biggest ever brick building. (It turned out it wasn't very secure.) And the time I got the idea of checking out which kinds of surfaces food would stick to when it was hurled strongly in their direction.

It was restful and interesting doing research. I particularly liked discovering the nature of water. The way it went straight through some things and stayed inside other things. The way it always fell to the floor when tipped out of a cup. The different kinds of splashes depending on what height objects were dropped into it from. Some of this water research seemed to attract approval from my parents, who would even on occasion organize me so that I could get on with it at the kitchen sink or in the bath. Some particularly interesting experiments I had to do when I could grab the chance, like throwing my little wooden dog at the washing machine door in the hope that the door would fall off. To understand this you need to know that I spent quite a lot of time watching the way the water moved in the washing machine. My Mum even put the machine on specially for me sometimes. And I really wanted to find out whether, if the door wasn't there, the water would stay spinning around inside, or spin out into the room.

I liked research, so being a one year old wasn't all bad, but there were some terrible indignities to be endured. Such as not being able to talk.

When I opened my mouth to say something all sorts of sounds came out, but not recognizable ones. My Mum seemed amazingly good at figuring out what I was trying to say, but it was such a clumsy and imprecise method of communication. I was determined to do better.

One day around this time my Mum took me to the park to feed the ducks. This was an outing I usually enjoyed. As soon as we got to the duck pond, all the ducks would abandon the people whose bread they were eating at the time, and come racing over to our side of the pond, as if they knew we had the best supply of goodies.

On this occasion my Mum bumped into a friend of hers, and once she had parked me in my pushchair, stood chatting with her. I wanted to chat too, but of course I could only make these annoying noises. I looked at the ducks. They were swimming around brightly, looking straight at me with their bright eyes, swimming past, then turning abruptly and swimming back in the opposite direction, still looking at me, strong and clear.

One in particular seemed to be keeping its eye on me. I watched it carefully. Then all of a sudden I felt sure I heard it say 'Have you got any bread today?'

I looked up at my Mum. Well, had we? Surely she wouldn't be so rude as to ignore the duck's question completely.

'She didn't understand,' said the duck. 'She doesn't know how to listen to us. I was speaking to you.'

To me? This was great. Someone was speaking to me. I tried waving my arms and letting out some of the sounds I could make.

'You don't have to do all that, you know,' said the duck. 'Just find me in your mind and then think your thought to me.'

This was not something I had tried. I'd never even thought of it. Thinking my thought to someone, anyone, let alone a duck on the duck pond.

I didn't really know what he meant by "find me in your mind" but I had a go. I imagined a picture of him in there, inside my head, a very tiny picture, and then I imagined I was tiny too, and was inside my head too, and I had to move back and forth, a bit like he was doing on the pond, until I found him.

Once I found him in there, I just sort of said my thought to him silently inside my head.

'Yes we have. It's in my Mum's bag.'

'Good. When will she remember to get it out do you think?'

'I don't know.'

I was very much excited by this exchange. It might not sound like much to you but you've got to remember I'd been out of my Mum for months now, and inside her for goodness knows how long before that, without one proper clear conversation with anybody. This was big stuff.

'Do you talk to everyone?' I thought to the duck.

'No. Very few. In fact nobody has been this way for years who knew how to speak with us. There was an old man once. You could tell he was the type, because all the animals in the park used to gather around him. You reminded me of him so I thought I'd try you.'

This seemed pretty odd to me, since I'd just been born, and was definitely not like any old man I'd ever seen. Still, I let it pass. This new friendship was too good to worry about something like that.

'Shall I try and get her to remember about the bread?'

'Yeah. That'd be good.'

I started to wave my arms and legs about vigorously and squirm in my pushchair harness. I added in a few sounds for luck.

'Oh goodness,' I heard my mother say to her friend, 'I forgot Zak. He'll be wanting to give the ducks some bread.' Have to give her her due - she's pretty smart at picking up the signals, even if she does forget me sometimes.

'Here you are Zak. Tear it in little pieces now,' and she went back to her conversation. Little pieces indeed! I was planning to give the whole lot to my new friend. Why tear it up first? I threw it in, rather a feeble throw, but it just made the water's edge, which was, I have to admit, only just in front of my pushchair. Anyway, my duck friend was able to reach it.

'Thanks,' he said as he towed it away. 'Maybe tear it up next time.'

*　　*　　*

As we left the park I looked with new interest at all the other animals and birds there. A squirrel ran up a tree. It seemed to halt for a second and look at me intently, but before I could find it in my head, it had rushed on up the trunk.

After this I developed a passion for going to the park, and soon had made friends with several pigeons, a goldfish in the pond, and two rabbits who were not very happy about being on display in a cage.

I wanted very much to talk to one of the squirrels, but somehow they didn't seem to like hanging around, and always darted off before I had time to get started.

But it was when I became friends with Maxine, our cat, that I really began to mind less that I couldn't talk with people yet, because Maxine was full of all sorts of interesting stories. I'd tell them to you, but we'll never get to the island if I do that - and I think what happens here on this island is even more interesting than Maxine's stories.

When I get back from here I'm certainly going to have some stories to tell her!

CHAPTER 5

My First and Last Day at School
age 5

When I was five I went to school.

My Dad took me in. I trotted along eagerly beside his big steps. People had told me school was going to be great, school was going to be fun - and I believed them. I was looking forward to it. Besides I could already read, and I'd even done a bit of writing, so there wasn't much else to learn.

I was keen to show off these skills, so once Dad had left, and I was let loose in the classroom with all the other kids, I went straight for the books. I gathered up quite a pile and sat down on the ground with them beside me. I took the first one and opened it on my lap. It was about a bird called Popinjay. I was disappointed how few words there were, but the pictures were nice, and it was a good story.

The next one I picked up was about electricity. I'd always found electricity pretty amazing, and had spent hours looking at the socket when the plug was out, waiting to see if I could see any of the electricity leaking out.

I was just getting to a really interesting bit about the power stations that make electricity, when the book was taken out of my hands.

'Oh, Zak. Don't you think you'd get on better with the book the right way up?' and it was returned to me the other way up. Now I couldn't read any of the writing.

I looked up blankly at the teacher, not sure why she should interfere like this, and turned the book back round.

'Now now, Zak. You'll confuse yourself later when you learn to read, if you get in the habit of holding books the wrong way up.'

Wrong? What was wrong about this way? It made sense to me.

'But I can read.'

'I don't think so, Zak. If you could read you'd be holding the book the other way up, wouldn't you?' she said in a sugary voice.

'Why?'

'Zak, now don't be rude. Just turn the book around please.' She suddenly didn't sound quite as nice. I got the feeling I'd better do as she said, although why was still a question I would have liked an answer to. I turned the book around and sat staring at the stupid pictures resentfully.

'That's much better Zak. Well done. Enjoy your book!' and she sailed off to another part of the classroom.

The only protest I could think of was to keep staring stubbornly at the same page. The rest of my stack of books sat beside me unopened. After all I couldn't read, could I, so there wasn't really any point in opening them.

Luckily it wasn't long before we went outside to play in the playground. I enjoyed this. Maybe school would be fun after all.

The next (and last) problem didn't arise until lunch time. The food smelled pretty good, and I was hungry. There was lots of noise in there, and when I'd found a place at a table with some of my new found friends I wanted to be sure they heard me, so I had to talk maybe a little louder than usual.

All of a sudden a dinner lady was staring down at me saying, 'You. Stop shouting at the top of your voice.' If she hadn't looked so stern

I'd have thought she was joking. The top of my voice. Did she really think this was the top of my voice?

To make the point that I wasn't shouting at the top of my voice I let out a real yell.

This wasn't a good idea. I didn't know yet the way things work in school. A rapid sequence of events saw me outside the head teacher's room. The dinner lady said the head teacher was kind, and she would help me settle down, but I was frazzled, and I had a feeling, as I was sitting there, that meeting the head teacher was something I'd rather avoid. I wondered if I could get my thoughts focused enough to fly off before she called me in. I closed my eyes and tried to concentrate. At first I couldn't. I was too confused. And the noise of the other kids playing outside distracted me. Then I managed to find my focus, and after half a minute I was able to open my eyes, (taking off with your eyes closed is not advisable), and I hovered slowly up into the horizontal position.

I was just getting my direction sorted out when the head teacher's door opened, and out she came.

I didn't know what to do. If I'd started trying to apologize or explain, I'd have plummeted to the ground. Although I didn't want to be rude, the memory of various other painful flying falls decided me. I started to move forwards, unfortunately in the direction of the staff room. Luckily (my luck again!) at that moment someone opened the door.

I recognised my teacher as soon as I entered. She didn't look stern now, so much as gasping, sort of like a fish short of air. Her eyes looked stiff, like a dead person. She wasn't making a very good job of holding her coffee cup properly to her mouth, and as I passed, her coffee all poured out onto her dress. There were quite a few others in there too. I couldn't afford to say excuse me or anything as I might have lost my concentration.

I noticed with relief that the window was open. If I could just keep steadily on course, I reckoned I would fit through the open gap nicely. As I was exiting I heard a loud thud and a crash that sounded like broken china, but I didn't look back

I flew straight on over the school railings and out onto the street. Once I was outside the school territory, I landed and ran off towards my house. Now that I was safely on my feet again, I could think about what had happened.

I felt a bit guilty for giving them all such a shock. I have to admit, I didn't actually understand why they found the sight of a five year old flying so devastating. I mean it's not like I'm an extra-terrestrial or a tyrannosaurus rex suddenly come to life.

Mum was at home when I got there. Her new job didn't start till the next week, and she was having a good clear out of the house before she got too busy.

She looked pretty surprised to see me, which I thought was unfair, as I was no longer even flying. I was just about to tell her what had happened when the phone rang.

'Hello . . . Yes, speaking . . . Yes, he's just come in the door . . . Oh, that's strange . . . I'm sorry to hear it . . . yes . . . I can manage that. All right, I'll see you at four. Are you sure you don't want to tell me more about it now, on the phone? . . . No . . . OK, well I'll be at the school at four then.'

In case you're wondering, I never went to school again.

CHAPTER 6

Magic at Breakfast
age 11
(five months ago)

For once we were all at breakfast at the same time.

'Pass the corn flakes Billy,' said Anna from the other side of the table.

Billy passed them without looking up or saying anything. Still, couldn't expect everything at once. Although we couldn't hear him, it was a rare thing to even see him at breakfast. He usually slept till the last minute and then raced out the door, late for school.

Mum and Dad were chatting in the kitchen making the coffee. I heard the clunk at the letter box as the postman stuffed our letters through. The number of letters we were getting seemed to increase daily. Mum said it was because we were getting lots of enquiries about their new holiday business and this was a good thing. Maybe soon we'd have to have a special postman just for us.

Anna, as usual, ran to the door to bring the letters in. She put them on the table in a heap, and I flipped through them to see if there were any interesting stamps.

'One from Canada,' I called out to no one in particular.

Dad was just coming in with the coffee. 'Let's see.'

He opened it, read it, and smiled a good big smile. 'Hey, Marion. We've got it!' Mum came in looking excited. 'We've got it. Look.'

'What have you got?' asked Billy. A miracle. He spoke. In fact two miracles. He spoke and it wasn't sarcastic.

'You remember the plan we told you all about, about renting an island in Canada for the summer? It's here. It's come through. We've got the booking.'

'We're going to rent a whole island?' I asked.

'Well, it's a very small island. There's only one house on it, and a cabin. So, yes, the island we rent is just for us - well, for us and the other family.'

'What other family?' Billy even looked up this time.

'The house is so big they have divided it into two. Another family will be renting the other half. The owner says here that they are called the Rosens, and they come every year. They've got two kids apparently, a boy called Sam, who's 12 - that'll be great for you Zak - and a girl called Leah. She's 8. Maybe you'll get along with her Anna.'

'Any teenagers by any remote chance?'

Sometimes I feel sorry for Billy. After all he is my brother. He told me once that when you're a teenager you don't want to be with your family so much, you want to be with your friends. No wonder he doesn't usually come to breakfast. Only family at breakfast!

'Uum . . . it doesn't say so. Sorry Billy. But the nearest town sounds pretty lively.'

'I thought it was a tiny uninhabited isle?' he said, only slightly sarcastic.

'It is. But it's a river island. It's in the middle of a huge river between Canada and the United States. There are lots of islands, hundreds, maybe even a thousand. And you get a boat with the house, so you can go across to the town whenever you want. In fact we thought we'd sign you and Anna up for the day camp.

'And me?' I asked. They knew I wouldn't want to go to camp. I'd had enough embarrassing times in public, when I'd done things that seemed normal to me, and people freaked out. I'd learned that I prefer my own company.

'Well Zak. There's a cabin there, that is like a big room, only a little way away from the house. We thought since you'll be on your own the most, you could have the cabin as your room. Maybe you can do some fun things in there.'

This sounded OK. Not definitely OK, but possibly OK.

'Living on an island is a great experience,' said Dad looking wistful. I knew he was remembering the island where he grew up in Greece. He always looked wistful when he remembered it. 'It's an experience I want you all to have. It changes you. You're never the same after living on an island.'

'I like how I am thanks.' (Billy again. Recognize him by now?)

'Oh Billy, just be positive for once,' said Mum, 'It'll be great. But I think you're all forgetting the time. We can talk about it more this evening. Hurry and eat up now.' Mum plonked some boiled eggs down on the table.

Anna looked up. 'Will you do your egg trick, Zak?'

Whenever we have eggs, Anna wants me to do my egg trick. It's just a silly magic trick, but she loves it. I think she really believes the egg disappears. She seems to think I can do any sort of magic I like, having seen me fly, and talk to our cat Maxine. I have to admit I am slightly her hero. The only problem is she sometimes tells her friends about what I can do, or even worse, her friends' parents. It's just because she's proud to have a brother who can fly. Luckily, the adults assume she's making it all up, but sometimes her friends pester me to show them. Mum and Dad are pretty strict about this, so I don't.

'Please,' said Anna.

'OK, just quickly.'

I grabbed an egg. I held it out in front of me between my thumb and forefinger. I swung it from side to side, turning my head to get a dramatic roll of my eyes as they followed the egg in its swinging arc.

'See this egg? It will disappear. When I say the magic words "Torgh N'Morgh" it will totally disappear. The only thing is, because this is a very special trick, I need someone else to help

me who believes in magic. Is there anyone here?'
Anna shot her hand up, as usual. 'Good. Now,
all the time I am doing the trick I want you
to say to yourself "The egg can disappear."
Ready?'

Anna nodded seriously, wide eyed.

'Right.' I waved both my arms about to
confuse her, slipped the egg into my right hand,
but kept looking at my left hand which was
closed, as if over an egg. I slipped the egg into
my pocket, and then, putting both hands above
the table dramatically opened my left hand that
I'd kept looking at all the time. Empty. Anna
clapped. Mum clapped. It was rather good. Even
though I knew it was a trick, somehow it seemed
to have something really magical about it. Funny
that.

'OK, now it's really time to move,' said Mum.
'Eat up Anna. Time to go in five minutes.'

When they'd all gone, Mum asked me what
I was going to do today. We usually made some
sort of a plan together in the morning. But since
all this post was coming, she was getting busier
all the time, replying to people who wanted to
have their holiday on Dad's boat in Greece.

I decided to stay at home for the morning and
do some drawing. Then after lunch I'd take a

trip to the Planetarium. Even though I'd seen the show countless times, it was still my favourite place to go. There was something so awesome about the darkness, and the starry, starry sky, and all those huge unimaginable planets whirling along with us around the sun. Why didn't they bump into us? Or just fly off, never to be seen again? It made me wonder whether there is some kind of giant pattern holding everything together.

CHAPTER 7

First Sight of River Island

still age 11

(By the way, from now on I won't write my age in the chapter headings because from here on the story is still happening - I mean I am still 11, and I am still on River Island now while I'm writing this, and the day when we arrived, that I am going to tell you about now, is only six weeks ago.)

We'd made it. Canada. Our summer holiday had begun. I was feeling really tired after the long flight and then the drive. But when I saw the river, I suddenly felt wide awake.

The water completely sparkled. The Thames water in London never looked like this, and I'd looked at it most days since I was born. It had a range, from greyish to greenish to brownish, and then startlingly, on very clear days, it was silvery blue.

But this was different. A bright, cheery, sparkly blue, with specks of gold dancing on it. It seemed so alive, so clear and inviting. I could see some small fish in it right there next to the quay.

'Come on Zak, here's our taxi,' called out Mum. She was getting into a small motor boat!

I knew we were getting a taxi to the island but all the time they'd talked about it I'd never realised it would be a boat taxi! I'd just assumed there would be a bridge across. But there were no bridges here. Just the town, the water front, and out in the middle of the river, some islands.

I wouldn't even have thought it was a river if they hadn't said so. Any river I'd ever seen you could see the other side. Not this one. It was huge. But then it didn't really look like the sea either. There were no big waves, and islands like that would never be in the sea. Islands with all kinds of trees, so small, and near each other, and without big rocky edges.

The rest of the family were in the boat looking at me. I jumped in carefully. Our luggage was all placed in the back near the taxi driver. Or maybe I'd better call him the boat-taxi driver. He looked as cheery as the river - relaxed, and grinning. Maybe it is a good job being a boat-taxi driver. Must put it in my very private list of good jobs. Owning a fish and chip shop, being an actor in Down Your Street, professional speed cyclist, writing joke books, boat-taxi driver. Maybe being a grown up isn't all bad.

'Zak, sit down, he's moving off.' My Mum was clasping her shoulder bag on her lap as if it would work as a life belt in case of sinking. She has a serious worrying streak, my Mum. She had her eye on Anna who was stretching over the edge of the boat, trying to touch the water.

The steady putting sound from the motor altered it's rhythm as the boat backed away from the quay. The driver had a skilful way of scooping the rope off the black, metal bollard thing. I swung my arm, copying the movement to memorize it for when I was older.

Then he put the boat into forward, turned the rudder, and we moved away from the roadside and off in the direction of the islands.

It seemed odd somehow to see the people on the street going in and out of shops, parking their cars and chatting as if nothing out of the ordinary had happened. To see them staying behind us, their noise not reaching us. And to think we were going to a place they couldn't walk or drive to, a place you could only get to by boat.

I turned and looked forward, over the pointed front of the boat. We were headed towards a cluster of about four islands.

'Which one's River Island?'

I'd addressed the question to Mum, but the taxi driver answered, 'That one on the left there'.

My heart jumped around inside my chest as I looked at it. Just a bit of land with lots of trees on it, almost like a forest.

'Doesn't look inhabited,' said Billy, in his practised monotone. I was sure he must practice it. It just wasn't natural to speak on one note like that. What's more, I can remember when he was younger he sounded just like everyone else. He must practice it in the bath.

All the same, his deader-than-a-rock face had slipped and he looked positively interested. I wondered if Mum had noticed this extraordinary feat. But he had his back to her.

'The house is just round the end there,' said the driver, 'You know you'll be able to see the United States from the other side of this island. This is one of the few you can see both shores from.'

We were getting close to the island now and

could see that there were clearings in the woods, and that the trees were oaks and fir trees and other kinds that we have in England too.

We rounded the corner of the island, and there it was - a big, grey, wooden house standing back from the water's edge. Across from it, maybe fifty steps away, and another wooden building, a bit like a large garden shed.

'There it is!' said Mum, letting out air for what seemed like the first time since we'd got into the boat. 'And there's your cabin, Zak.'

My cabin. My very own cabin. I could hardly wait as the taxi man hooked us up to the bollard and turned off the engine.

Mum was getting up, holding Anna's hand. Billy was just sitting there gazing into space. I leapt the gap from the boat to the wooden platform and sprinted down the path to the cabin.

CHAPTER 8

My Cabin

It was brilliant. It was ace. It was it. It was what I'd always wanted.

As soon as I rushed in the door I could see it was perfect. Even before I rushed in. I'd already taken in walls made of grey logs neatly connected at the corners, the way there was a slightly trodden path to the door, the trees close around it. I seemed to know it. It was what I had dreamed.

The inside was one big space. with hardly anything in it. There was a table and chair near one window, a worn out armchair, a sort of sofa made out of an old mattress and some cushions, and a huge cupboard with a battered tape player in it. Up the far end, covering about a third of the room, was a platform that was high enough that even if someone jumped they couldn't reach it. It was built across the whole width of the cabin, sort of inserted in the walls. There was a ladder up to it. I scrambled up the ladder and there, at the top, on the platform, was a bed - a big mattress on the floor.

Wonderful. Perfect. I rolled onto the bed and lay on my back, arms and legs outstretched, eyes open, grinning. I'd arrived. I laughed out loud.

*   *   *

The next day, while Mum went into the town in our little motor boat to get some supplies, I set about improving the cabin. Even though it was perfect, it could still do with some improvements. In fact part of it being perfect was that I could change it around a bit, and make it how I wanted it to be, how it had never been before - mine.

I'd found some thick rope coiled up in the attic of the house, and Mum had said I could use it for something. It was perfect for a rope ladder, and I set about making one. Half way through making it, I got inspired to make the platform totally private by taking away the wooden ladder and having a rope one instead, that I could pull up after me.

What next? Across the roof of the cabin was a huge round beam. It was like an entire tree. Somehow I got the idea of making a trapeze, maybe because the beam was in the perfect position. I could see I'd be able to climb up the ladder to my platform, holding the special pulling-rope that would dangle from the trapeze to the ground, just like in the circus.

It only took me a couple of days to make it. It would have been quicker but I had to persuade Mum to let me use the broom handle.

I was ready to try it out. I hauled it up to the platform and teetered on the edge holding the broom handle. One . . two . . three . . and jumped. I was swinging.

The first time I did it I could only swing four or five times before my arms were totally too tired to keep holding on. Then I discovered the first law of trapeze riding: "The only way off is down". I looked down and tried to choose a moment when I wasn't above the armchair. I did miss it, but even so it was not a comfortable landing. So I pushed the armchair away, dragged the old sofa-mattress across and put it underneath the landing area. That was much better. Who needs a sofa anyway?

Now this was getting really good. Get ahold of the pulling rope. Climb up onto the platform. Haul up the trapeze. Grab it. Stand right on the edge of the platform. One, two, three - leap into the air (holding the trapeze of course). Swing madly for about forty seconds, and plummet down right onto the lumpy old mattress. Perfect. Now all I needed was a little technique and some stamina, and I could join the circus.

* * *

I really enjoyed finding places in my cabin for all my special things I'd brought from London. Mum had suggested we pack some things each that were not too big, but reminded us of home. I'd chosen my stuffed gorilla Cando and my old trainers that I'd almost completely worn out. Those trainers and I had gone millions of miles around London together. I tied the laces together and hung them around a nail on the wall. They hung nicely there. They really made me feel like I lived here.

I'd brought two books with me, *Tintin in Tibet* and *My Friend Mr Leaky*. When I'd been ill with the chicken pox Dad had taken some time off work and read Mr Leaky aloud to me from start to finish three times. We had laughed a lot together - it's a pretty funny book - and it's one of those books you can read again every two months. And whenever I read it I always remember the nice feeling of Dad sitting on my bed spending time with me, and us laughing.

Then I'd brought my knitting needles of course. Knitting is one of my favourite ways of spending time. It's just so amazing that something can start off as one long thread and end up as a piece of material, just by wiggling it around on two sticks. I wish all of life were so easy! Imagine if to make food you just took a seed or two and some soil and sort of stirred them around for a while and then you had a potato. Well I suppose that is a bit what happens come to think of it, except for the time factor - you have to leave the potato in the ground for a certain amount of time, but then there's a time factor in knitting too. The more time you spend the longer it gets. And I want mine to get a lot longer. I'm going for 3,243 miles which is the exact distance from where we are here on the island, to our house in London. I measured it when we first heard we were going to Canada. I was worried about going so far away from home, so Mum showed me where it was on the map. And I measured it.

I also brought Scrabble. It's a game I really like. Possibly because my name is the highest scoring three letter word. I like the way the words interlace more and more the more you play, and that one word is also part of another word. Come to think of it, it's a bit like knitting, isn't it?

At the bottom of my bag I was surprised to find my favourite tape of flamenco music. I'd been searching for it for months, back home in London. It must have been in the bag all along. I was eager to hear it again, so I put it on, very loud, and stamped it's dance, and sang that kind of flamenco-shouting-singing, all around my cabin. Now I felt totally at home.

CHAPTER 9

Laloune and the Zing

The first time I met Laloune was the third evening. By now I had got used to the area around my cabin, and wanted to explore the rest of the island. I set off in the afternoon and stayed out for hours.

It was beginning to get dark, and I was just deciding to go back when an owl landed on a branch above my head.

I sat very still. It sat still too, except for turning its head.

Well, I thought, I'd better get to know the creatures here. I wondered if they would talk with me. Even though I knew the animals in England would talk with me, I wasn't sure whether things might be different so far from home.

'Fine evening, isn't it?'

'Yes. I believe it is.'

'Oh good. I wasn't sure if you were going to understand me.'

'Not hard at all. You communicate very clearly. How did you learn?'

'Well, I suppose you could say a duck taught me.'

'Few people learn. Most never even try. Those who do give up too easily.'

'Do you know other people who communicate with creatures then? I've never met anyone else who could.'

'There are some. Not many. Far and few between. People who have the time. And the imagination.'

'Well, I've just arrived here for the summer. I've got lots of time. My name is Zak, by the way. What is yours?'

'Laloune. Pleased to meet you. You'll like it here. Not like that brother of yours!'

'You know him?'

'I've seen him. He's the sort to think a place like this is dead and boring - nothing to do. I doubt he'll even notice us. But for someone like you this island is paradise. So much for you to learn. So many of us for you to meet. Such a magical spirit here. You see, we only have to share the island with people in the summer months. In the winter the whole river freezes over, and nobody stays. So we can build up the zing again.'

Laloune seemed to like to talk. And it was interesting talk. 'What zing?'

'The zing you feel when nature has it's own way. It is woven by the moving creatures, and respected by all. Each thread of it is very delicate. It needs to be allowed to grow till it gets thick enough to be strong. But it is invisible to most people. They don't realize they have to adjust their tone so as not to break it. They just walk straight through it, carrying on their loud conversations, and destroy it without even noticing. Just like walking through a cobweb.'

'Oh no, that's terrible.'

'Yes it is. But here we are lucky. At least we can re-weave it in the winter, when all the people go away and the river freezes over. If you want I'll take you to a place where the zing is strong enough that you might be able to see and feel it.'

I hesitated. This was a bit quick for me. How did I know whether to trust this owl? How did I know what she would lead me into? What was zing anyway? Would it do me harm?

But I liked the feel of Laloune. She didn't seem like one who would lead me into trouble. Anyway, "time for an adventure" as my Dad was always saying.

'Yes, yes I would like that,' I communicated.

'Follow me.'

Laloune took off with a lovely swing of her silent wings. How could they be so strong and so gentle at the same time?

I jumped up and followed her.

She led me into the thickest part of the wood. I hadn't come this way on my explorations yet. The undergrowth was a bit prickly, and I didn't want to get scratched.

'OK, steady now. In order not to destroy the zing you need to soften your edges. Can you do that?'

'Soften my edges? Like this?'

Laloune laughed as I drooped and let my head flop.

'No no, not like that. Keep your body up, but soften round the edges, a bit out from your body - soften there.'

I wasn't too sure what Laloune meant. How could I soften where I wasn't? Laloune seemed to realize I was stuck.

'Imagine you have feathers. Long soft ones. They stream out from your body into the area around you, don't they? Just fluff them up, and keep them loose. Feel how soft they are.'

I thought of the robin who used to come to our garden in the winter and puff his red breast out.

'Like that?'

'That's it. You're getting it. I think that'll be OK.'

I walked around a bit, imagining my feathers. They were white, long and super soft. I could almost feel them gently stroking my skin.

'I like this!' I laughed, 'Will they keep me warm too?'

'Not too fast!' chuckled Laloune. 'Now. Remember what we came for. There is some well woven zing about ten feet in front of you. Walk forwards very slowly and see if you can feel it. You won't damage it because you are soft now.'

I edged forwards. I felt the light wind passing through my new white feathers. After several steps I felt something like a thread across my path.

'Is this it?'

'You're doing better than I expected,' said Laloune. 'It is a bit of the weaving, but you haven't got to the denser part yet.'

'But won't I damage it if I go through?'

'No, no. It's not a solid thread. It's an atmosphere. I can't pluck your feathers, can I, because you have created them with your mind. But I could disturb your mind so that you wouldn't be able to imagine your feathers any more. That way I could destroy them. It's the same with the zing. It's not a physical thing, so it's the way you think that affects it. The way you think makes you soft or jagged. As long as you respect the zing's atmosphere you can't damage it. But if you are jagged all around you, instead of soft, you'll destroy it instantly.'

I understood. Sort of. Enough to try it. I paused a moment to check I was still soft around me. Feathers there? Yup!

I walked forwards and felt the moment when I passed through the thread. It seemed to let me pass without snapping or even sagging. It was springy and very light.

A few steps later I virtually crashed into the denser zing.

'Wow, Laloune. This is wild. It's so strong! Why did you make it so strong just here?'

'Because there is something through there we wish to protect.'

'What?'

'I can't tell you without consulting the other creatures.'

'Can't I go in there?'

'No. Anyway, the zing might harm you. When it is this dense, it is actually harmful to humans, unless they are prepared.'

'But I've got my feathers.'

'Even so. You would need more than feathers to go in there.'

'Why do you make something that's harmful to us?'

'To protect life. So many humans haven't learned how to be sensitive. They'd just blunder on through any special spot, not notice it, and destroy it's atmosphere with theirs. But even when they pay no attention to nature's atmosphere, they still pay attention to their own feelings if they are strong enough. When people come this way, they start to feel strange. Sometimes they feel spooked, or they suddenly feel faint or extra tired. Sometimes they feel sick. It's not long before they decide to go back. That way at least our special place is left in peace. And although they don't know it, that's better for the people too.'

'Laloune, may I come back here with you

another time? Not to go into your special place, but just to be here with you? I like it here.'

'Of course. I'm often out flying at this time of night. I'll come by your cabin one evening soon. There's a lot more I'd like to show you on this island.'

I said goodbye to Laloune and walked back to my cabin. I felt happy. Quiet and happy. Just full and quiet and happy.

CHAPTER 10

Seeing the Shine

A few days later I was sitting outside my cabin looking at the stars through my binoculars. It always amazed me how through a perfectly ordinary pair of binoculars the stars suddenly shine and become colourful. Some are red, some blue, others seem to shift and twinkle much more than you'd expect.

Even though there was a lot of light from the full moon I could see quite a few constellations - Taurus the Bull with its horns, Gemini with it's two twin stars Castor and Pollux, and Leo the Lion looking so proud lying there with his head held high.

It was quite a clear night and I could even see the Pleiades really well. Somehow they always look on a different scale to other constellations, like they are millions of light years further away. I was imagining being out there among them. It was silent but songful. I could move extra fast because there was no air resistance or friction, and I zoomed merrily from one of the stars of the Pleiades to another. I was making a five pointed star in space, weaving the stars together with my dance.

I was disturbed from my star weaving by a nearby rustle of leaves, and an owl hooting.

I looked over to the trees and could just make out a dark owl-sized blob.

'Laloune, is that you?'

'Yes. Can you come out with me tonight?'

I jumped up. 'You bet! Where are we going?'

'Don't ask - just come.'

'OK. One thing though. I know how to fly. Can I fly there with you?'

'You are an unusual one. Well, let's give it a try then.'

'Can you wait a few minutes? I have to change my clothes - these are too flappy. And then I need to concentrate. And another thing - I don't fly very fast, so you might have to stop and wait for me once in a while.'

'I can wait. Off you go then and get ready.'

I ran inside to put on my pyjamas. They were

the smoothest, closest fitting clothes I had with me. Perfect for flying. I'd discovered in the past that it was no good trying to fly in loose or flapping clothes - they dragged me down. Whoever invented Superman clearly didn't realize this technicality when they gave him his cloak.

I went back out, found a nice spot under the stars and started to concentrate. My attention became very still and wide. I became aware of the water shining in the moonlight and lapping on the boat mooring quay with my right eye, and of the rough, curvy logs of my cabin with my left eye. Straight ahead were the scraggly pine trees among which Laloune was perched.

I felt my energy change, the weight beginning to pour out of my legs. I tried to stay relaxed even though I felt really excited. Relaxed was the best and only way to take off. No point in making an effort to take off. Wouldn't get anywhere that way. Just breath quietly, relax, let it work, let my intention organize me . . .

The weight was sliding out of me fast now, any minute now that last bit would whoosh out, propelling me on my way.

Whoosh - it was more powerful than I expected. I shot upwards, and in my shock only just remembered to turn horizontal before it was too late. Once I was horizontal it was like there was a cushion of air underneath me, and I stayed up nicely, hovering just level with the tops of some big bushes.

'I'm up,' I called out to Laloune.

'I know. I see well at night.'

'Oh, of course you do. I can't see you though. How do I find you?'

'I'm here,' and Laloune swept past. I'd love to be able to do that nice rhythmical swooping kind of flying, but I'd tried it once and crashed instantly. I have to be satisfied with the steady, straight line approach.

'Come on then. Stop dreaming and follow me.'

I started up, and soon was cruising along behind Laloune's lovely, silent flap of the wing.

It was wild, cruising through the trees on the island with Laloune. All my flying up to now had been done in a city. OK the River Thames was exciting to cross, but I could only do it on foggy nights, or my parents would never live it down with the neighbours. So this was something new. Really free flying. The wind ruffled my hair and felt warm as we wove our way between the trees.

'Almost there,' said Laloune. 'We're going in here. Careful of the narrow bit.'

I followed Laloune between the almost touching branches of two big trees, in time to see her land on a branch. Looking down to find a place to land I saw we were in a clearing - and gathered in the clearing were several small animals. I landed as gracefully as I could (didn't want to be shown up for one of those clumsy humans) and looked around more carefully. Sitting quite still were several squirrels and a tiny wood mouse.

'These are the beings who have agreed to take care of the island this summer,' explained Laloune.

'We are having our full moon meeting. The squirrels are the stewards of the island. And this mouse is our protector for the year. I am the messenger who keeps everyone up to date on what is happening on the island. I put forward your request to enter the area where the zing is thickest and so they asked if they could meet you.

'Animals, this is Zak. He knows our talk. He knows about being soft to enter the zing without harm. I taught him. He is a a quick student. Ready for more I would say. He can also fly.'

The way she said it, I could feel Laloune was pleased to have found me, and to be introducing me to the animals. She sounded almost proud.

'Hello,' I said, not quite sure how to live up to the impression Laloune was giving of me.

'We hear you want to visit the protected area.'

The mouse had a surprisingly strong and authoritative way of communicating.

'Well, yes. I would like to. Laloune explained it to me, and . . .'

'Do you realize the responsibility this will place on your shoulders?'

'Um, no,' I thought I'd better be honest.

'Once you are given the secret of how to penetrate the zing, you will have a particular power few humans have. A wrong action could destroy something very precious.'

Not another power, I thought. Do I really want this? I was used to the others. I'd had them all my life. Of course I had fun with them, but they were just part of being me - I hadn't chosen them. And sometimes it had been a burden to me, being so different. Sure, I really wanted to go to the special place Laloune had showed me - but this seemed to be turning into something serious . . .

'I realize,' I said suddenly, rather before I had decided. I was startled how solemn I sounded - like when people make those oaths at weddings.

'The protection we will give you for this zing

will, to some extent, protect you in them all. But never make the assumption it is enough. Always keep alert, and if at any time you feel uncomfortable, pull back. There are some places on the planet still so uninvaded by humans that the zing is extraordinarily strong. If at any time you come to one of those, I do not suppose this protection would be enough.

'Now, please be good enough to wait a minute. We have to find out about you.'

The mouse signaled to all the squirrels, and they gathered closer together, crowding in around me. Laloune flew down from her branch to join them.

I assumed they would ask me questions, but instead they all went very quiet and very still. For a whole, long, silent, minute.

Suddenly they all murmured at once. They seemed to assent to something, and then moved out again into their original places.

The mouse said, 'We have decided to grant you the special favour of protection to visit the zing. Your age and your flying ability counted in your favour in our decision. And our feeling of your character. Come over here.'

It seemed odd as I walked towards the mouse that he could be so small and at the same time so powerful.

'Please sit on the earth. Close your eyes. We will give you the protection you will need.'

I sat with my eyes closed wondering what would happen. I admit I was a little scared.

I felt a sort of delicate breeze coming around me, as if people were blowing gently on me from all directions - and yet none of them was big enough to reach my whole body like that. I was tempted to open my eyes to see what was going on, but I feared if I showed myself to be a cheating sort of person they would not give me the protection. So I kept them shut.

'Now it is time for you to visit the protected site. Although you will eventually be able to go on your own, for this, your first visit, some of us will accompany you. Laloune will lead the way, but we would like you to stay earth connected. Sh'krump, who is to become your daytime companion, will lead you on the ground. I will follow behind to check the atmosphere.'

I stood up. I felt a bit shaky with everything being so unfamiliar.

Laloune took off and the squirrel Sh'krump signaled to me to follow him with a flick of his tail.

We went through the woods. I realised we

were in a part that wasn't familiar to me. I followed Sh'krump for a while. He seemed to go in a twisting and turning route. Maybe so I wouldn't be able to find the way by myself later, I thought. We arrived at the place where Laloune and I had stopped the time before.

I felt nervous. The mouse said. 'We cannot proceed unless you can talk yourself out of your fears. We will wait here until you settle your attitude. It is not too late to return the gift of protection if you find you cannot enter.'

The animals sat down - Laloune on her branch, and Sh'krump and the mouse on the ground near me. I felt dazed. I sat down too and closed my eyes. I could feel the breeze again, and the nice springy solidity of the forest floor under me.

There was a really peaceful feeling here. Alive but at rest. It occurred to me that these trees had been here without moving for twenty or thirty years. Why move? It was good to be still, to rest. I liked the smells and the feeling of the earth under me. I felt safe.

As soon as I felt this I surprised myself by standing up. My eyes were still closed. I breathed deeply, and felt myself expand, as if I grew several centimetres in all directions.

The ground still felt solid and good under my feet. My legs felt really strong, almost rooted into the ground. Maybe this was what the trees felt like.

I opened my eyes and noticed straight away the shine. Had the moon come out from behind the clouds while I was sitting?

'Good,' I heard the mouse say. 'You are ready.'

Ready for what? I didn't feel the need to move at all, maybe I wouldn't need to move for forty years like the trees. It was so peaceful to be still.

'You can go in now. Follow Sh'krump.'

Sh'krump started off, very slowly towards where I had experienced the thick zing. I followed. After all that was what I had come here for, and considering the trouble the animals had taken over me, it seemed wrong to stop here. I told myself I could come back and stand with the trees another time.

As I walked forwards the branches seemed to part. I felt the first thread of zing that I had felt before. I paused, checked my feathers were really fluffy and soft, and continued.

'Good,' said the mouse. 'Now for the next step.'

Sh'krump continued forwards, and I followed him. I felt almost as if I was sleep walking. The stillness of the pause had stayed with me even though I was moving. It was a very weird sensation.

Step by step the zing got thicker. I thought of my protection and felt the threads slide away as I went through them. Laloune was up above, Sh'krump ahead, and the mouse behind. I felt like a creature too. I was one of them, an animal. I moved silently, gracefully. I was alert.

The trees thickened and it was a bit hard to push through between their branches. Clearly no creature my size had been this way before. Then after the thickest bit they opened out suddenly into a clearing. I couldn't believe my eyes. The shine was almost dazzling, almost too bright to look at.

I followed Sh'krump to the middle of the clearing. I could hear music. It sounded far away and close at the same time. Sublime. With singing voices. The sort of music I'd always imagined angels singing.

As I stood there I noticed that the shine had a sort of prism effect at the edges. It broke up into colours, like a rainbow. There was a rainbow around each tree and bush. There was even a rainbow around Sh'krump, and when I turned to look at the mouse, sure enough there was one around him too.

I walked a few more steps to the centre of the clearing. and sat down. Now this was somewhere I really could stay for forty years. It was so beautiful. The colours were soft and bright at the same time. The way they shimmered and moved made them seem alive.

I reached out my hand to see if I could feel the rainbow prism around a bush near to me, and was surprised to see the colours even around my own hand.

'This is amazing,' I said. 'Is this what you protect, this light and the singing sound?'

'That is only part of it. You cannot experience everything that is here yet. But yes, the light and the singing are important.'

'But why is it like this?' I asked, waving my hand around to enjoy the coloured patterns it made.

'It is a place of unspoilt energy, where the zing has been built up and woven for hundreds of years by the animals of the island. The same could happen anywhere where there was a sufficient respect and understanding of nature. As Laloune told you, it is usually the humans who destroy it. Of course they don't realize they are destroying it. It just gets trampled and broken by their way of being in nature, and by their beliefs and attitudes.'

'What else is here that I can't see? How can there be things here that I can't see?'

'There are things everywhere that you can't, or don't, see. The difference is that here you are more likely to see them, because the power of the zing can work on you to increase the range of your sensitivity.'

'Can't you tell me what they are, what to look for?'

'No. It wouldn't make any difference. When you are ready you will find out.'

'Will I be ready today?'

'There's no knowing. You might be ready today, you might never be ready.'

'Can I do anything to speed it up?'

'Yes. You can be quiet. Deeply quiet.'

I sat. I was quiet. After all, what could you say to that? To ask another question would be to be unquiet. To be unquiet would be to slow the process down. So I was quiet. I sat. And I watched.

The shining light and prisms were still there. After a bit I thought I could see a pulse in them too. What were the other things I wondered? What did Laloune mean they are there all the time only I can't see them? How can there be things here I can't see? I've had my eyes tested and they are as good as eyes get apparently. So surely I must be seeing everything?

I lost track of time. Had I been here an hour, two hours, or just ten minutes? I looked at my watch, but that was no use, as it always stopped when I flew. I never figured out why. Perhaps it needed some sort of connection to the ground for the battery to work.

I began to feel tired. The colours didn't seem so bright now. My legs were going numb and I felt restless.

'Time to be going,' said the mouse. 'It is as important to recognize when it is time to leave as it is to keep yourself soft as you arrive. Until you can recognize the right leaving time you are only to come here with one of us.'

I stood up. Actually I was glad to leave. It was all getting a bit much for me and the idea of getting back to my cabin and crawling into my bed was really delicious.

I wished I could be there immediately without having to trudge home through the woods.

I made my way out of the clearing and back through the thick part of the bushes and trees. Once I was out, Laloune appeared on a branch. 'Flying home?'

'I don't think so. I'm too tired to get started.'

'Want an escort?'

'Yes please.' To know Laloune would be flying along above me was very comforting and my step picked up a bit of spring.

I said goodbye and thank you to the mouse and Sh'krump, and walked in a daze back to my cabin. Laloune flew on slightly ahead, and when I arrived she was perched up on her branch, exactly where she had been when the adventure started.

I said goodbye to Laloune, who swooped off into the night. I stumbled though the door, climbed up to my bed, and fell asleep as soon as my head hit the pillow.

CHAPTER 11

Unexpected Power

I know my Mum means well but sometimes her good ideas backfire. Like when she suggested I do a magic show for Anna's birthday party.

We'd been on the island a week now. Billy and Anna were off each day making friends at the day camp. Mum was anxious to get me involved with the other children. She couldn't seem to understand that I was happier being on the island on my own than going with the others every day to the town. But then she didn't know about Laloune and Sh'krump and the zing, did she?

Anyway, she always has this idea of supporting people's natural interests. I suppose that's why she bought Billy that electric guitar - not that he ever touched it. Just as well or we'd have all had to buy ear plugs.

So one morning, in fact just the day after I was introduced to the strong zing, Mum came back from shopping in the town with a magic set for me.

'Zak, it's Anna's birthday tomorrow and she's invited some of her new friends. Would you do a magic show for them? I'm sure they'd love it. You're so good at that sort of thing.'

I had to admit, though of course only to myself, that I am rather good at that sort of thing. I couldn't wait to rush back to my cabin and tear open the magic set and get started.

'Oh, just remembered something I need to be getting on with. See you Mum!' I said as I ran out the door, clutching the magic set under my arm, before she had time to ask me to help unpack the groceries.

Two minutes later I was already immersed in the instruction book. The set had a disappearing handkerchief trick, some plastic rings to join together, and four other really good tricks which I won't tell you about yet or it'll spoil the party!

I spent the rest of the day practising, and by the following day I was ready for the party. The kids were arriving at four. Mum had organized some games for them. Then they would eat.

Then, the climax of the party would be my magic show.

I felt a bit sick, performers nerves maybe, and couldn't really join in the tea, which was a pity as there was the best chocolate mint cake that Mum only makes for birthdays.

Sam and Leah, the kids staying in the other part of the house, were there. We hadn't really got to know them yet. Sam was always indoors playing on his computer, and Leah, well, Mum said she seemed a bit aloof and kept herself to herself. But Mum said we had to invite them. I didn't see why. Sam spent most of the party stuffing himself with our goodies, and Leah was sort of drifting around not talking to anyone.

Then Mum gave me the signal that it was almost time for my show, so I sneaked off to get ready. I put on the red cloak Mum had made for me out of a bedspread, and some thick black tights she had bought specially. We'd had a laugh cutting the feet and some of the legs off, to make them fit me.

I set up the fold-away card table, put Mum's purple shiny scarf on it and began to lay out my tricks.

Mum put her head around the door to check that I was ready (you bet) and called the kids in. Boy, they were noisy - but I was pleased to find that as they entered the darkened room and saw me standing strong and impressive behind the magic table, they were awed into whispers.

Once they were all more or less settled I began. I switched on the tape I'd set ready at some eastern sounding music. After about half a minute I turned it down low and said, in the mysterious and commanding voice I'd practised in the bath, 'I am Jadu, the most famous of magicians. I only come to earth to do a magic show once every hundred years. Pay attention and watch well. You will see real magic in front of your very eyes. You will see things that when you tell of them, no one will believe you. Attend!'

The first trick was a pretty easy one, but it worked well, and they genuinely seemed amazed when the scarf disappeared.

Then it was the magic balls. This requires a lot of concentration, because if I lose my place, the whole trick is given away.

'I've seen this one before,' called out a superior sounding voice.

Thanks a lot Sam. You try and do it then.

I managed it, but not without a moment of panic that I was going to move the wrong container, and the secret of the trick would be revealed.

The next trick was the "changing the colour of the water" one. I liked this one, and felt confident enough to look around at them as I was doing it. I was surprised to notice Leah, sitting slightly apart, watching really carefully. Not like Anna's friends, who were in open-mouthed awe. You could see Leah was thinking. Not nasty, put-down thoughts like her brother. She was thinking inside thoughts, her own thoughts, thoughts that might even have had to do with magic.

The water went from pink to purple to orange to green and all the six year olds clapped and laughed. Sam leaned against the door post sneering slightly and making a point of looking bored. Leah didn't clap or laugh with the others. She just went on thinking.

Just then Mum came in having cleared up the tea. 'Are you going to do the disappearing egg one, Zak?'

The disappearing egg one. I hadn't thought of that.

'I've brought you an egg to use.'

Mum passed me an egg. It was slightly warm. She must have boiled it specially.

I started my spiel.

'And now, the great Jadu will show you a trick that took years to perfect. Pay attention for the fabulous egg trick!'

I rolled up my sleeves, and took the egg between my thumb and forefinger. I held it in front of me dramatically, and turning my head so that I could look out of the corner of my eyes I swung the egg in a wide arc in front of the audience.

'This egg, which you can all see, which has only just been boiled, will, at the moment I say the magic word "Torgh N'Morgh" totally disappear. I will not hide it. I will not ask you to look away. It will just disappear from in front of your very eyes. But being extra strong magic, it can only work if somebody else believes in it. Is there anybody here who believes this egg is going to disappear?'

Two of Anna's little friends shot their hands up. Sam put his hand out with his thumb turned down - thanks a lot Sam, you really help the spirit of the party.

'OK. What are your names?'

'Sylvia'.

'Mary'.

'OK. Sylvia and Mary please keep saying to

yourselves, "The egg can disappear" while I do the spell. At the moment I say the magic word "Torgh N'Morgh" the egg will disappear.'

The mysterious eastern music had finished, and something more jolly was next on the tape. It wasn't the right atmosphere. I turned it off, and was surprised how silent the room was. Everyone was waiting to see what would happen. Nobody spoke. Nobody moved. Only Sam shuffled about a bit.

'Start now, Sylvia and Mary.'

I picked up the magic cloth in my left hand, and waved it about, drawing it over the egg.

I began muttering the words I was making up for a spell. 'Koja amhast pintell mundee. Phnellac, shnellac, spellac, kree.'

As I said these words my arms started to feel weird, they were buzzing as if they were full of electricity. My hands buzzed the most of all. I felt sick again. Maybe I was getting the flu? Better get this over with and have a rest.

'OK, Sylvia and Mary? Concentrating?'

While talking I had been whirling my arms to confuse people, so that I could swoop my empty left hand forwards, and slide the egg quietly into my pocket with my right hand, but things started going differently. Both my arms lifted up in front of me as if by themselves. Both hands were palm up and totally open. The egg was there for all to see in my right hand. This was crazy. I'd never pull the trick off this way. But I couldn't stop. It was as if my arms were doing it all by themselves. And I was saying the words too. I could feel I was going to say the magic word any second. This was crazy. Embarrassing.

'OK, Sylvia and Mary,' I heard myself say, 'This is it. Torgh N'Morgh!'

At that instant the feeling in my arms got really strong, so strong I couldn't move. I felt rooted to the spot. A whoosh of energy that felt like the lightening had hit me passed through my entire body. I watched powerless as the egg disappeared off my hand. It just disappeared, right in front of my eyes. Just went. One moment it was there, the next moment it wasn't. Anna's friends were laughing and clapping as they had for the other tricks. Sam's jaw had dropped. Leah was smiling slightly.

I felt badly sick, bowed quickly and rushed out of the room to the toilet. I sat down on the toilet seat and shook.

I felt confused and lost. I hardly knew where I was.

How could the egg have disappeared? It

just couldn't.

I put my hand in my pocket half expecting to find it. It wasn't there. Perhaps I'd put it in the left pocket by mistake? No.

I held my hands up and looked at them. They looked normal, but my right hand felt strange, the skin was sharply sore, almost as if it had been burned just where the egg had been.

If this was real magic I wasn't sure I liked it. I felt scared. Disconcerted. If the egg could really disappear, what else might happen?

CHAPTER 12

Sh'krump Explains a Few Things

I still felt odd when I woke up the next morning.
I hadn't slept well, dreaming of things disappearing
- my old trainers, even my cabin disappeared in
that night of fevered dreams.

I couldn't face going for breakfast in the big
house, and maybe bumping into Sam or Leah,
or having to listen to Anna saying how great
the egg trick was. So as soon as I got up, I went
out to see if I could find my animal friends. Life
seemed simpler with them than with people, at
the moment.

I remembered the mouse had said Sh'krump
would be my daytime companion. But we hadn't
set up a rendezvous or anything. I wasn't sure
how to find him. So I just walked in the
direction of the zing place, hoping I'd come

across him.

It wasn't long before I heard a chittering above me in the trees. I looked around. 'Sh'krump, is that you?'

'Yes, here I am.'

'That's great! I was just looking for you.'

'I know.'

'You know?'

'Of course. I have been appointed as your daytime companion, so it's up to me to stay in touch with you. I know where you are, and what is going on with you, from dawn to dusk.'

'That's weird! Do you know what happened to me yesterday then?'

'Well, I don't see exactly what you are doing. I more feel your mood, and I know your location. So I know that you were in the house, and you had some kind of a shock. What did happen? It certainly felt very strong to me.'

'Yes . . . strong . . . I don't know . . . I'm not sure you'd understand. The egg disappeared.'

'The egg?'

'Yes, the egg in the magic trick.'

'Oh you were playing with magic! That can be dangerous!'

'No, no, not real magic Sh'krump. Just a magic kit my Mum got me. For kids, you know. And

I did my old egg trick. I've done it loads of times, but it was just pretend magic. It never went like this before!'

'So tell me exactly what happened.'

'Well, I was doing the trick, and instead of me putting the egg in my pocket, it was like my arms took on a life of their own, and the egg actually disappeared. That's what it seemed like. I still can't believe it.'

'And what about just before it disappeared?'

'Well, I was feeling sick, and then something like a huge electric shock, like lightening or something, went through me. And then my hand burned a bit, and . . . '

'Zak. There's something I need you to listen to, and listen carefully. It seems that your visit to the zing has put you in a state of power. In this state, your thoughts are more likely to come true, than previously. You will need to be careful what you think.'

'What do you mean?'

'Well, when this happened were you thinking about the egg disappearing?'

'Of course. That's the whole point! I got other people to think about it too. But only as part of the build up!'

'What you need to realize is that when you

thought it, so clearly and strongly, your energy was arranged in such a way that it actually happened. Can you understand that?'

'I don't know. You mean visiting the zing actually changed me in some way? Like now I have some kind of power I didn't have before?'

'Yes. So it seems. It isn't always like that, but you must have been ready. I suppose the signs were there - you can already fly, and talk with us. We should perhaps have foreseen this. Now, did I understand you right, that others joined in and thought about the egg disappearing?'

'Yes.'

'Well then, maybe you are only beginning. The beginning of power shows when you think very hard about something, along with others who also have some power, and then it happens. Who was thinking with you?'

'Two friends of Anna - Sylvia and Mary.'

'No one else?'

'Well, I suppose anyone else might have been thinking too. If they'd wanted to.'

'Let's try an experiment. You think of it raining, as hard as you thought of that egg disappearing, OK?'

'But it's not even cloudy!'

'Please try it Zak. It needs to be a really

concentrated thought, so keep it going as long as you can.'

'OK.' I thought as hard as I could of rain coming, for at least two minutes.

'Can I stop now? It's getting tiring.'

'Yes. That'll do for now.' Sh'krump stared intently at the sky for what seemed like a long time. He turned back to me, 'No rain. I'm glad to say it seems that you are only beginning. At this stage you still need to think with others to affect life. This is nature's safeguard.'

I felt relieved that I wasn't going to have every little thought come true! I'd read enough stories about people who could have their wishes come true, and who wished by mistake for some stupid thing that caused complete mayhem, to know just how hazardous this power could be!

But I was also upset. I hadn't expected everything to change like this. I wanted to calm down, to be soothed. I thought of the peace of the zing spot. I'd like to go there again. But what if it gave me more power? I didn't know what to do.

'Zak,' Sh'krump was still there - I'd gone so deep into my reverie I'd forgotten him.

'Yes.'

'There's something I need your help with. It's

to do with Sam.'

'Sam?'

'Yes. He has been setting a trap for the animals on the island. I want your help to stop him.'

'A trap? What do you mean?'

'He found an old-fashioned animal trap - you know, the kind with springs and teeth - in the cellar of the big house. He has been setting it in various places around the island. Yesterday one of the squirrels got caught. It was terrible to see.'

'Oh no!'

'What's more he has come close to some of our special places, and we are worried he is going to destroy the zing.'

'That's terrible!'

'It's a lot more terrible than I can even explain.'

'What can we do?'

'Well, you could use your new powers of thinking, but you need some help. How about you make friends with Leah? She would be useful in this.'

'Leah! But she's only eight! And she's a girl! And she doesn't even talk to anyone. No, I don't want to make friends with her.'

'Well, you think of a way then. But please come up with a suggestion soon.' Sh'krump flicked his tail sharply, and darted off into the trees.

I didn't think we'd finished the conversation and was a bit surprised he left so quickly. What could I do about Sam? I didn't even know him! Surely his mum ought to be the one to stop him. But maybe she didn't know he was doing it. If I could just think hard enough, maybe she'd find out, and then she would stop him. Yes, I decided to try that . . . I closed my eyes . . .

After a few minutes trying to imagine the exact moment she would find out about Sam and the trap, I felt tired. I wanted to curl up and sleep and forget all about it. Besides, it was clouding over, and looked like it might rain. So I started back to my cabin. By the time I got there, the first few drops were falling.

CHAPTER 13

Not Nowhere

I have this habit. On rainy days I like to get
into bed, and dig down under my covers, like
my pet mouse Jipper used to do when he was
making his nest. I have a special torch I keep
inside my bed in case of midnight emergencies.
I find my torch, grab a book from the stack
Mum has brought home from the library, and
start reading. I have been known to read the
whole thing before I come out. (Mum chooses
pretty good books, luckily.)

When I'm in this mood I get right into the
story and forget everything else. It's like floating
away from my normal life on a raft - I drift
out into the middle of the ocean where there is
nothing, no person, no other boats, not even any
land in sight, just whatever is in the book. I

forget where I am, what day of the week it is, what time of day it is. I even forget who I am sometimes.

I got into this habit in London, where there's no messy bit of nature where I can just go outside and mess around in the rain, you know, digging muddy holes and getting soaked to the skin without even noticing. So when it rains I've got used to going inside instead of outside - in to my room, in to my bed, in to my book. Then I'm away. Sometimes for hours.

What I'm going to say next isn't something I've heard anyone ever talking about, but I'm hoping you will know what I mean. I feel a bit nervous telling you about it, in case it turns out I'm the only one who has this experience, and you'll think I'm crazy. Oh well, here goes . . .

Once I get into my inside world it seems very real. As real as the outside world. Sometimes I wonder which is more real - the world out there that everyone I know is walking around in, or the world in here, in me, I don't quite know where, but somewhere in me, not out there anyway, but somewhere else - but not nowhere.

I've realised that this not-nowhere world is where I am all the time I am thinking, and I've noticed (have you ever noticed this?) that I'm always thinking in here.

Since I first noticed how much thinking I am doing I have been out to catch myself by surprise at some moment of NOT thinking. But every time I jump out unexpected on myself, there I am thinking. Pretty ordinary things quite often, like "When is my friend going to come over?" or "I'm hungry, what shall I eat?" But not always. Sometimes I'm having really wild conversations in here between me and . . . I don't know who . . . me, I suppose. In these conversations I invent things, wonderful gadgets for saving peoples lives, or for avoiding the boring work in boring activities like filling baked bean cans. Or I talk to world heroes - Magic Johnson or Tom Hanks or Oprah Winfrey or famous dead people like Abraham Lincoln or the wisest ever medicine woman from the Blackfoot tribe. They have some pretty neat things to say. They even give me advice sometimes, when I am stuck on something, like what to get my mother for her birthday. Last year Abraham Lincoln suggested I get her socks. He even told me what colour. Pink! I was sceptical, but I didn't have a better idea. When I went to the sock shop they had some pretty cheap (but nice of course) pink ones. So I got them. It was amazing. Mum was beside herself. She said she'd been exactly wanting some pink socks since she'd seen a film two months ago where the main character had pink socks. She kissed me all over - too much actually. Next time maybe I'll get her blue socks.

Anyway, if you don't have this kind of inside world conversation, I recommend it. It's a lot more vivid than the best graphics on your computer, and the whole conversation is directed personally at you.

So I developed this habit in London, of going to the not-nowhere world on rainy days. And on this particular day when I got back to my cabin after my conversation with Sh'krump about the egg disappearing and it was just beginning to rain, I felt homesick for London. So I climbed up my rope ladder, pulled it up behind me for total and guaranteed privacy, curled up under my covers even though it wasn't cold at all, with my book and my torch, and started reading . . . . so when I noticed a scratching on the window pane I had absolutely no idea how long it might have been going on for.

I unfurled my rope ladder and clambered down it. 'Must put up a straightforward rope that I can just slide down when I'm in a hurry,' my inside voice said. 'Not a bad idea,' I agreed.

At the window, to my surprise, was Sh'krump. He was scratching hard. I threw it open and he started communicating straight away.

'Zak, you've got to come. There's trouble. I need your help.'

'What is it? What's happened?'

'I'd better explain as we go along. There's no time to lose. A disaster. More than a disaster.'

I jumped into my shoes and rushed out the door after Sh'krump.

The rain was belting down. While I'd been in my not nowhere world, this somewhere world had really got a storm going. The wind was strong - not steady strong, but pushing in great gusts. The rain was almost horizontal and stung against my arms and legs. It was difficult to walk and difficult to see.

Sh'krump leaped on ahead of me, pausing only to let me almost catch up, and then bounding on. I yelled after him, 'What's going on Sh'krump?'

'I can't tell you. I can't explain. You'll have to see for yourself, Zak.'

He seemed to be going to the back bay of the island.

I was worried. 'Has something happened to Billy, or Anna?'

'No, no, not them. It's . . . .' Sh'krump's communication was swept away by a gust of wind and I couldn't catch the vital information. Who then? Leah? Sam? Surely in a storm like this they would have stayed at home. Maybe it was one of the animals in trouble.

It was all I could do to keep up with Sh'krump. The ground was slippery with the rain, and he was darting along from tree to tree at top speed. I couldn't manage to communicate at the same time as keeping upright and keeping running. So I didn't try asking any more questions. Wait and see.

Then, when we were nearly at the edge of the island, I heard a terrible sound - a long, low, loud, groaning. It sounded like some trees grinding and rubbing against each other in the wind. But it seemed to be coming from the water.

I wasn't too sure about going any closer and was just about to consult with Sh'krump when I saw the most terrifying thing I have ever seen or imagined in my entire life, rising up at the water's edge.

It was a monster, a huge dark monster, standing up almost like a person, only twice as high, and so wide, as wide as the biggest sumo wrestler I'd ever seen. Its arms were thick, its neck short, its heavy head hanging forward of its back. It was dark greeny black all over, covered in large slimy scales. It had almost human-like hands, only four times the size. They looked like they could grip and crush anything. It opened its huge black mouth and let out a roar that made the ground shake.

I froze solid, my arms went stiff, and my legs jammed into the ground like rocks. But my eyes were still working. I could see it clearly through the undergrowth. It was bellowing its head off. Even through the roar of the storm it was an awful sound, like the sound a mother elephant might make if she'd seen her children killed by a hunter. It seemed to be pulling at its leg as if it was stuck in the water.

Sh'krump was chattering to me from the tree.

'We must help it, Zak. It's in terrible pain.'

It was in pain all right. The sound of it ripped though me, hard to bear, like the collective pain of the whole universe. I couldn't help myself wanting to do something to help it. No creature should be in that kind of pain. But I was doubtful whether I could even take half a step nearer it, whether I could even move one muscle.

Sh'krump kept running up and down the trunk of the tree.

'Sh'krump for God's sake stop acting so hyper. We've got to think,' I said, surprised at my own voice of command.

The monster was roaring its head off. You'd think it was trying to out do the storm, and all other monsters that ever existed, dead or alive, in every movie ever made. Maybe any real ones that it knew of that existed somewhere too.

As I stood frozen to the spot, watching, I noticed to my amazement that I'd started thinking quite sensibly about what to do. No point in rushing in to ask a roaring monster what the matter is when you don't know it, it doesn't know you, you probably don't speak the same language, it's three times your size and it's gruesomely scaly.

As I was thinking this the monster managed to pull one leg up out of the water. There was something stuck around it's leg. It waved it frantically in the air. Then I realised. The monster must have trodden in one of Sam's traps.

'Zak, you've got to free it.'

'Free it? You mean you want that creature free on the island? Wouldn't it be better to leave it trapped? Trapping it seems like it could be the best thing that could happen.'

'My God! No, Zak. It must be free. It helps

people. It's essential.'

'Essential, are you crazy?'

But Sh'krump wasn't listening to me. He seemed more and more agitated.

'I'll have a word with it first to explain what's going on.'

'No Sh'krump, it'll kill you with one swipe!'

Before I could stop him he had darted down the tree and across to the boat. The storm was still loud, so I couldn't catch a word he was saying. It was even hard to see him through the fast driving rain. But I saw the monster notice Sh'krump, and it didn't hit out. It seemed to be listening to him, not killing him.

I could tell from the way Sh'krump's tail was switching back and forth that he was communicating.

But I didn't have long to think about it. Sh'krump came rushing back.

'I think it's understood. It's in a lot of pain so it wasn't taking everything in. Go and free its foot. Go carefully and whatever you do, if you care for your life, don't behave like a nightmare! I can't explain now. Just don't behave like anybody's nightmare.'

Sh'krump must have lost it. He wasn't making sense. Great. Fine. OK. Just free this monster please, and if you care for your life, don't behave like a nightmare. Piece of cake. Anyone would do it.

But for some reason there didn't seem to be any real alternative, and I felt myself beginning to move.

I stepped out from behind the branches, trying to seem as calm and friendly and cheerful as nobody's nightmare could ever have been. It wasn't easy. I felt the muscles in my stomach gripping so tight that I could hardly breath.

I started to approach the water's edge. Just then a huge gust of wind came and flung me forward. I caught my foot on a rock and fell right into the water. Sitting there, I looked up at the monster, just inches away. It was looking down at me, and through it's howling I received loud and clear the message, 'Get this thing off my leg'.

I looked at what it had on its leg. It was an old fashioned animal trap. Revolting. The metal teeth were set on a powerful spring that right now was clamping deep into the flesh of the monster's leg. I felt really sorry for the monster. Green and scaly or not, it didn't deserve this fate. God, Sam was a pig. Imagine ever wanting to catch any creature in one of those.

I tried to indicate to the monster to hold still while I loosened the catch. I was afraid of getting my hand caught. The spring was strong and it might flick back on to me. The trap wasn't designed for anything as big as a monster's leg, which made it hard to undo. I pulled and squeezed at it, hoping I had the strength to push the spring enough to open it, hoping the monster wouldn't demolish me while I was struggling here at its feet. I was shaking and sweating with the strain of the situation. The storm howled around me. Then, as I struggled, suddenly the catch came loose and the trap opened. The monster immediately stopped its fearful groan and started to whimper.

It looked down at me for a moment - and I was surprised to see deep gratitude in its eyes. Then it clambered out of the water and limped softly off into the forest.

I sat in the water, shaking and feeling sick. While I was undoing the trap I hadn't had time to react. But now I felt freaked out by the gruesome feel of the monster's slimy, scaly skin, wrapped over that terrifying power I could feel in it's limbs. I had never felt anything like it. It was like a combination of the rhinoceros I had once had a chance to put my hand on at the

London Zoo and those kind of slimy rubbery toys you can throw at walls and stick to them. Only worse. Much worse.

Sh'krump came over and encouraged me to get up and get out of the water. My legs felt wobbly but I was sore and cold and wanted to move, so I managed to stagger after Sh'krump to where I could sit on a tree trunk.

CHAPTER 14

The Nightmare Monster

After sitting in a daze for a few minutes I realized Sh'krump was communicating something.

'Thank you, Zak, thank you. I don't know what we would have done if you hadn't been here to call on. I can hardly imagine what a disaster it would have been if our monster had been caught.'

'Our monster? You know this monster?'

'Oh yes. It lives underground in the woods.'

'You're joking. It lives here, on the island?'

'Yes, it's always been here. Longer than any of us. It keeps itself to itself, staying in its hole most of the daytime.'

'Thanks a lot. Why didn't you ever tell me about it? I mean, I could have run into it at any moment. I might have died from the shock!'

'There were other things to talk about. Anyway you were very unlikely to run into it. It's a master of camouflage. No human has ever knowingly seen it. It's odd, it doesn't usually make mistakes. That's why I called you.'

'It is?'

'Because we had to get the monster out of there before anyone saw it.'

'But I saw it.'

'Yes, but you're different, so people don't take you seriously. If you tell them about it they'll just dismiss it as your fantasy. But if they saw it themselves . . . '

'What would happen?'

'They'd never understand that the monster is here to help them.'

'It is?'

'Yes. It's a nightmare monster. But most human beings wouldn't know a nightmare monster if they saw one. They'd probably destroy it.'

Sh'krump seemed to think this would explain everything. It didn't.

'Sh'krump, what is a nightmare monster?'

'If it wasn't here people's nightmares wouldn't just be dreams. They would become real!'

'What are you talking about?'

'The second someone starts dreaming a dream,

whether it's a nice dream or a nasty one, that dream starts moving towards reality. It's a natural law of creation. First it's in your mind. Then it starts to become real. Of course it can take a long time, and lots of things don't make it all the way through because they conflict with other dreams you've had, and that creates a sort of jammed up tangle. But nightmares are really dangerous because they are so powerful that they can break through the tangle. Thank goodness for the nightmare monster!'

'But what can it do?'

'As soon as somone starts having a nightmare the monster sets off to try and make friends with it. It has to listen to the nightmare in a special way. Then the nightmare doesn't harm anyone. But if no one is there to listen to it, a nightmare can turn very nasty and destroy our world.'

Sh'krump was getting really worked up. I'd never seen him like this. And he sounded really serious.

'Every nightmare is trying to send a message. But no one is getting it. They just hate the nightmares. Then the nightmares get worse and worse. And people hate them more. This is really dangerous. People have no idea how dangerous this is!'

I didn't manage to take this in. I was wondering which would be harder - to make friends with the nightmare monster, or to make friends with a nightmare.

So I asked Sh'krump, 'But who would make friends with a horrible, slimy monster?'

'That's just the point. That's why the monster has to be so scary looking. It's scariness makes the nightmares respect it. And right away they feel at home with it because it looks like one of them!'

'So they talk to it?'

'Not necessarily. Not all nightmares know how to talk. But the monster knows how to get their message anyway, without words. Then the nightmare calms down. All it needs is for someone to get it's message!'

'So the monster just has to get the message and then everything's all right?'

'No, not quite. It also has to deliver the message, otherwise the nightmare would come back after a while. The message has to get to a person and become something new, something that will help someone. So the monster still has some work to do. Luckily it knows how to give the message to a person as a good idea. Once someone gets the idea, that nightmare will never come back any more.'

'You mean like when I get an idea to invent something?'

'Yes, something that will help people.'

'Like a great new kind of fire escape, or plastic bottles that dissolve after you use them, or . . . .'

'Or just a new idea of what you could say to get someone to understand you.'

'Wow. The monster does all that! It works hard.'

'Yes, very hard.'

'It must get really hungry! What does it eat?' My bones went ice cold as a horrible and frightening idea occurred to me. 'Does it eat children?'

'No no, not children. It eats zing.'

I suddenly felt dizzy and weird. Maybe it was the mention of the zing. How could it eat zing? Precious zing! My head was spinning. I was almost crying - I was so relieved that I wouldn't be eaten.

Sh'krump didn't seem to notice what was going on with me. He kept on chattering, 'I mean, it doesn't eat zing like you and I eat food. It's more like it eats what zing gives off, it's special atmosphere. So when it eats, there is as much zing there afterwards as there was before. It's like smelling a flower, or like breathing. But with it's whole body. It knows how to breathe in the zing atmosphere through every pore of it's skin and that perks it up and gives it all the energy it needs. So now you know, Zak, why it would be so disastrous if Sam destroys the zing. And why you've got the help us stop him. I didn't want to tell you before, but now you can see, Zak . . . Zak?'

Sh'krump trailed off as he saw how pale and floppy I was.

'Zak . . . are you all right?'

I wasn't all right. This was enough for me for one day. I was dazed, cold and hungry, and didn't know which way was up, or whether dreams were real or reality was a dream. Sh'krump led me home. As we made our way across the island all the nightmares I had ever had swirled through my mind, and I saw the nightmare monster coming gently to get their messages.

CHAPTER 15

Taken by Surprise

I spent the next few days taking it easy and getting to know Sh'krump and Laloune. As dusk fell each day Sh'krump, my daytime companion, would leave me, and when I was through with eating I would go out and find Laloune and go flying with her.

Sh'krump turned out to be a lot of fun to be with. He showed me the best spots on the island for swimming and we went climbing trees together. I began to think the rest of the summer might be more like the kind of holiday I was expecting.

And he was really understanding. I was worried about Sam's traps, but I wasn't in the mood to do anything else heroic. I was still shaky after the whole monster episode and just wanted to forget about it and enjoy myself. Sh'krump asked me again to make friends with Leah, but when I reminded him why I didn't want to, he let it drop. Apparently Sam hadn't set the trap again anyway, since the squirrel got caught.

On this day I am going to tell you about now, I woke up feeling more like my bright and cheery self again, and set off for the clearing where I'd been meeting Sh'krump each day.

When I got there, sure enough, there was Sh'krump to greet me.

I noticed how good it felt to see him. It was like a veil was lifting from my mind that I didn't even know was there. I could stop thinking, and just be. Be with my new friend. Because he was my friend. Better than any human friend I'd ever known. With him I felt comfortable. With him I could be myself. Maybe it was because he didn't expect anything of me. And he didn't think there was anything peculiar about my powers. He told me that each creature has its own different set of powers that equip it to live it's life, and he never questioned mine.

'Hi Sh'krump!' I called out, 'It's good to see you.'

'Hi!' said Sh'krump, 'You too. Want to come and climb trees?'

'You bet.'

I'd been climbing with Sh'krump the last few days, and knew how fast and far he could go. I didn't want to get left behind if I could help it, so I rushed over to where he was.

Sh'krump set off up the tree, gripping the bark with his sharp claws. I was jealous of those claws, and of the strength of his little leg muscles.

We were climbing an old oak tree with deep grooves in the twisty bark - which helped me get a grip with my trainers. I launched myself upwards. I felt unusually nimble when I climbed with Sh'krump - my arms stretched out of my back like elastic as my hands reached for the branches to haul me up. My legs bent extra far, making it easier to reach the next branch. It was fun. It was brilliant. I felt light and free.

Sh'krump stopped a little way ahead, half way out along a branch. 'I'm going this way,' he said, indicating a route down his branch, with a big leap to a branch in the next tree. 'Can you?'

No. I was sure I couldn't. Nobody could. No human that is. The branch would bend too much, and I couldn't possibly leap from it anywhere except straight down.

'I'll have to go down and up again. Will you wait for me?' I felt disappointed. When I felt so light and free I didn't want to remember that I was still a human.

'Come this way,' said a voice, quite close by. 'There's a way across here.'

'Oh, thanks, where are you?' I called out, and then I realised that I was speaking aloud, in human speech, and that the reason I was doing this was that I had been spoken to that way. Had one of the animals learned to speak like a person?

'How do you know human speech?' I called out into the branches to the side of me, from which the voice had come. It flashed through my mind that perhaps I was talking to an escaped parrot.

'I'll tell you when you get here,' laughed the speaker.

'I can't see the way.'

'Look out!'

A thick rope hit me across my arm. It so startled me that I almost fell off the branch. It had swung across from the tree that Sh'krump was jumping over to.

'What do I do?'

'Just hold on and swing.'

For some reason I trusted this voice. I grabbed firmly ahold of the rope, and, after a moment's hesitation, leapt off my branch, hollering like Tarzan, 'Wooooaaay. Here I come.'

The rope swung long and far, like the brilliant rope swing at my aunt's house. I careered at considerable speed towards the other tree. Just as I was about to crash into a thickly leaved branch, it was pulled aside, and I swung through and landed in a heap on a wooden platform next to, of all the creatures on the planet, Leah! Leah who I'd hardly spoken to in the whole time we'd been here. Leah, who I'd always assumed was only into girl's things. Leah who was only eight. She was sitting there, laughing. She wasn't laughing at me. Her laughter was OK. It was fun laughter. It was the kind of laughter you can't help joining in with. So I did.

When we'd calmed down a bit, I looked around, and the more I saw, the more I was amazed.

'Is this yours?' I asked her.

'All mine. Totally mine. You're the first human being who has ever been here except for me.'

'But how did you make it?'

'Just sawing and hammering. There's plenty of wood around.'

'Yes, but how did you know how?'

'I watched my mother and father doing jobs

around the house. It's not hard.'

Leah had made herself an extraordinary tree house. There were slats of wood attached to the main trunk, like a step ladder, leading up and down to more platforms. Each platform was skilfully woven into the surrounding branches, and looked really secure.

Some of the platforms were very private looking, with walls of planks around them, with holes cut in them for windows, and even window blinds made of woven rush mats. I really wanted to look around! I wondered if she would let me explore it later. Better be nice to her.

'What do you do here?'

'My own things,' said Leah. 'And I watch the animals . . . and you.'

'You've been watching me?' I was flabbergasted. 'Since when?'

'Since you started coming here. You're very interesting to watch.' For the first time since I'd met her, Leah seemed a little shy. 'I hope you don't mind. I didn't plan it that way. The tree house was already built when you arrived. I made it last year. You see we come here every summer.'

I felt stunned. How could Leah have been here, first, in this most special place of mine, the place that I thought was just for me and the animals, the place where I felt completely away from people. It ruined it.

'You've ruined it,' I said. 'You've ruined this place for me. I didn't come here to be spied on you know.'

Leah looked upset, horribly upset. God, what would I do now? I didn't want her running home crying and telling the others.

'Look, Leah. It's just that this is, well it's a sort of secret of mine, coming here, and I thought no one else knew about it, and I thought I was alone, and it's a shock to find you here, and, and . . . you've been watching everything.'

It suddenly occurred to me that she might indeed have been watching everything. Everything. The conversations with Sh'krump and Laloune. My flying. What had she seen? And had she told anyone?

'Leah, it's very important that you don't tell anyone. Does anyone else come here with you?'

'Never!'

The way she said it, I knew it was true, and I also knew she could keep a secret better than anyone I'd ever met.

Just then, we heard a scrabbling on the tree

trunk above us, and Sh'krump appeared, laughing.

'So, you two finally met!'

'Oh, stop it, Sh'krump,' said Leah.

'Now now, don't get tetchy Leah. You'll survive this intrusion into your private world, you know. Zak's one of us.'

One of us! What did he mean, one of us? What a nerve. To think that I could be one of anybody. The most self evident thing about me was that I was unique. Everybody said so. My mother was always saying so. "You know Zak," she would say, "there is nobody else quite like you. Of course that's true of everybody, but it's truer of you" and "I wonder how I produced you Zak? You don't seem like the rest of us."

'What do you mean, one of us?' I asked Sh'krump, indignant.

'I mean you know, Zak. At least you know how to communicate. It's true there's a lot you don't know, mainly because you never thought to ask. But don't worry, Leah and I will teach you.'

Leah, I thought to myself, teach me! Oh, sure. I suppose Leah can fly can she?

'No, I can't,' said Leah. 'But I know other things.'

Wait a minute. She was answering a question

114

I hadn't asked. Not aloud. Had I? Maybe I had said it aloud without realizing. I must have.

'No, you didn't,' said Leah.

'Didn't what?'

'Didn't say it aloud. You didn't say your thoughts aloud.'

'So how come you're answering? Look Leah, if I didn't say it aloud, you wouldn't be answering me, would you?'

'But I did.'

'Did what?'

'I did answer your thoughts, didn't I?'

'But how do I know I didn't say them aloud? People do that sometimes you know - say their thoughts aloud without meaning to.'

'So you're telling me you can't tell when you speak aloud and when you don't?'

She had me. But wait, if Leah could read people's thoughts surely someone would have told us, her brother Sam, or her mother, or someone? She must be lying, or have some kind of clever tricky way of doing it.

'Don't believe me then!' said Leah, sounding really annoyed.

I realised with a start that I was reacting just the way people react when they discover one of my powers. They never believe me. They assume

I am lying, maybe trying to seem big or show off or something. I hate being so misunderstood. It's this kind of thing that leads me to keep my powers secret. Maybe Leah could tell what I was thinking. Why not? It wouldn't be any more strange than flying. But it was. It was more strange. Flying is quite normal really when you think about it - birds fly, airplanes fly, even balls fly for a while - but what object or creature is there on the planet that can read someone's thoughts? Perhaps Leah was a really a witch, or an elf.

'Don't be silly. Of course I'm not,' said Leah, 'And I'm also not the only one who can do it. Maybe even you could do it.'

Even me! Surely especially me. As an insider to the world of special powers, it must be something I could do easily. I mean, if Leah could do it.

'Have you tried to teach anyone before?' I asked her.

'No. Sh'krump didn't think I was ready. I suppose now he does - since he said we could teach you things. I've seen you fly. If I teach you how to hear people's thoughts, will you teach me how to fly?'

'How to fly! Nobody but me can fly.'

'Why not?'

'Because they can't. Because I'm unique, weird, different. You've got to be born different to do it. It wasn't something I learned, you know. I was born flying.'

'Prig!'

'What?'

'Nothing. Where's Sh'krump. I think it's time he took you back to your cabin. This was a stupid idea to let you find me here. I should never have listened to him! Sh'krump . . . Sh'krump! Zak says he's the only one who can fly. He thinks he's different. I don't want to teach him anything, I wish he hadn't ever come here.'

After that Leah refused to talk to me until I apologized for being so big headed and assuming she wouldn't be able to do what I could do. I was pretty curious to learn to read people's thoughts, and began to think, why not see if Leah could fly? It might even be fun to go flying together. And I certainly wanted to spend more time in her splendid tree house. So I apologized. And thus began my friendship with Leah.

CHAPTER 16

Sam's Reality

I admit meeting Leah made me reconsider my attitude to people. I mean she was so different from what I had assumed. It even occurred to me that Sam might be worth making friends with. So one day when I saw him hanging around the big house after lunch I tried to have a real conversation with him.

'Did you know there is a monster on this island, Sam?'

'Oh yeah, and there are piranhas in the river too.'

'No really. I saw it.'

'Well I saw a monster on this island myself actually.'

I was startled. Did Sam already know about the nightmare monster?

'He tears the limbs off anyone who gets in his way. You can see the blood dripping out of their arm and leg sockets after he drops them.'

'You saw that?'

'Yeah, sometimes twenty thousand times a day, Zak. He's one of the bosses in my new computer game.'

'Oh!' I wasn't specially interested in hearing about Sam's computer game right now. I wanted to talk about something real.

'You should come in and play it, Zak. It's wicked. You can select whether the game just leaves the bodies strewn all over the road bleeding, or have a vulture come and eat them. The graphics are amazing.'

'Sounds great,' I muttered weakly. I'm not much of a one for blood. Even on the screen it makes me feel peculiar inside.

'So what does your monster do?' asked Sam, 'What's he like?'

'Well he's really big, about three times as big as us, and he's sort of dark slimy green, and . . . . . .'

'Yeah, and he smokes Camel cigarettes, I know.'

'No, really Sam, he's the most yukky thing to touch, sticky and scaly, and cold, with slime like,

like snot, all over him.'

'Woah, wait a minute, that's gross Zak. Don't make me throw up.'

'And when he moves his scaly skin sort of creaks and groans, and . . . .'

'Good sound effects there Zak!'

'. . and the thing that's the most amazing about him is that if you get to know him, he is really gentle.'

'Gentle?'

'Yeah, he's not threatening at all, not angry, not about to eat anyone. In fact apparently he helps people.'

'He does?'

'Yeah, he, you know, he sorts out their worst dreams. I mean he saves them from their nightmares.'

'I could do with him. Can you send him over? I have nightmares every night.'

Every night! I was astonished. 'What kind of thing?' I asked.

'Oh, often it's Bing and Bong. They're not even from a shoot-em-up. They're from a pin ball.'

'A pin ball?'

'Yeah, you know, a pin ball game. I've got this wicked one, and instead of balls there are these two poor suckers Bing and Bong stuck in a pin ball machine that is millions of times as big as them, and you can make them bounce around in there. Some of the bouncers have spikes on, some have flames coming out of them. When they hit those killer ones you get bonus points. My highest score is 635,982. The cool thing is Bing and Bong actually move, you know they have bodies, and when you get them near one of those spike or flame bouncers they actually curl up and look like they are trying to avoid it, and when you get a direct hit, they make this amazing contorted grimace expression, and groan and scream like crazy. You should see it Zak. We could play it tomorrow if you want to come over.'

I didn't want to. I wanted to be with Sh'krump and Leah tomorrow. But I couldn't exactly tell Sam that.

'So what happens in the dream?' I asked, to avoid his invitation.

'Well I'm in the kitchen, and I hear a crashing sound and when I turn around it's my computer smashed open on the floor.'

'That's your nightmare?'

'That's not even the worst of it, although I always feel sick when I see that part, but that's not what's so scary.

'So then what happens?'

'So then it turns out that the pinball game was loaded when the computer breaks, and Bing and Bong escape when the screen shatters, and they are out to get me. I run like hell and they chase and chase me. I know if they catch me they're going to do something terrible. I run till I'm exhausted, then I trip over something and they are just about to catch up with me when I wake up.'

'You mean you have this dream often?'

'Most nights. That's why I'm so knackered all the time. I've been awake half the night. I don't dare go back to sleep while it's dark, because Bing and Bong might be there waiting to pounce on me. Sounds stupid, I know, but it's really scary. I get them back for it though, in the day. Yesterday I paused the game just at the point where they were both hitting the spiked buttons. Ha! Left the suckers like that for two hours!'

CHAPTER 17

Midnight Crisis

Leah had finally talked me into teaching her to fly. We'd agreed to meet at midnight to get started.

As I waited for Leah to come I went outside my cabin to get a feel of the night. You could see from the way the clouds were moving fast across the stars that there was quite a wind. It wasn't the ideal night for flying. If it had just been me wondering whether to go out I would have turned around and gotten deep under my covers and stayed there.

What's more, there was definitely an eerie feeling around. I'd go so far as to say, in retrospect, that the night was suggesting that we'd be better off in bed. And we would have been, at least if we'd all been in bed. As it was, maybe it was a good thing Leah came over, and I didn't just bury my head under the covers.

I heard the cracking of some twigs as someone, and I was glad to see it was Leah, approached.

'Hi,' she whispered.

'Hi,' I whispered back.

'Well, are you ready to show me flying now?'

'Yeah, I guess so.'

I realised we were whispering, and couldn't quite figure out why, but it seemed a sort of mark of respect for the night, and our not so usual place in it.

'What do I do?'

This was a difficult question to answer. I suddenly realised I didn't really know how to teach someone to fly. 'Well, first just stand there for a bit, sort of quietening down. Get very still.'

'Like this?'

Leah was standing facing the scraggly pine trees.

'OK, now take three deep breaths . . . OK . . . now concentrate.' Leah furrowed her brow. 'No, not like that! You'll never take off if you're trying so hard. I mean just be alert, really alert and kind of let go of everything you normally think.'

Leah was very still now, and silent. I thought

she might be ready.

'OK. Now sort of let the weight slide out of your legs. It has to slide out so that you are light enough to take off.'

'Like this?' I couldn't see any change in Leah, but then would I be able to see her weight sliding around inside her body?

'I don't know. Maybe. Keep trying for a bit and we'll find out.'

'I think it's happening,' said Leah, 'I feel weird and light and, oh . . . I think its happening. How do you keep your balance?'

'You steer with your head.'

'With your head?'

'Yes. Just think where you want your head to go and your body will follow it, like a high diver, or a trampolinist.'

'OK. Shall I think my head to go up then?'

'Yeah, you could.'

Just at that moment, just when we thought Leah was about to take off, we heard a terrible, heart stopping scream from the woods.

'Zak. What was that?'

'I don't know. Something bad.'

It came again.

We looked at each other, frozen with fear. I didn't have to be a mind reader to know that

Leah was wondering just like me - do we dive for cover, or ought we to go and see what it is?

Suddenly I heard an owl's call, that was familiar to me by now. It was Laloune.

'Laloune. Did you hear that? What is it?'

'Come quick!' was all Laloune said, then she took off again and started flying towards the woods.

Our decision was made. Leah and I took off towards the woods at a run.

Laloune was leading us towards the place of strong zing. As we approached the screaming increased and then stopped abruptly. The silence was almost more scary then the screams.

I thought of the nightmare monster. Was it him again? Was he really so harmless if he could scream like that? What if he had screamed to tempt us out, and now he was laughing to himself in silence, waiting for us to get near enough that he could leap out and grab us? Maybe Sh'krump was wrong. Maybe he didn't just live on zing. Maybe he did eat children . . . . .

'Leah, Leah!'

She was running on ahead of me.

'What?' she puffed.

'Leah, watch out, there's a monster living here. It might be out to get us.'

'Don't talk rubbish Zak. Why would Laloune want us to be eaten by a monster. Look there she is.'

I'd forgotten Laloune. I'd been running along behind Leah in such a panic that I'd forgotten everything except my fears.

Leah had been following Laloune all the way. Laloune settled on a branch. 'Here,' she said.

My skin went all prickly as I wondered what we'd find. Leah went ahead.

'Look over there, there Zak. Oh no. It's a person. It's . . . it's Sam! Zak, it's Sam! He's not moving! Oh Zak, he's dead!'

I stopped. Sam was lying on the ground motionless. His back was towards us. His ankle was in a trap - his animal trap. There was a great pool of blood all around him. I froze. What could we do? We were too late. Sam must have been screaming from the pain, and then he had died. He'd died just a few minutes ago. My whole world seemed to spin and dive into darkness. Nothing made sense. Nothing made sense. How could Sam have died?

I sat down.

'Aren't you going to do anything?' asked Leah.

'He's my brother. We've got to free him.'

'But he's dead. We're too late.'

'Zak, for God's sake. We've got to free him. Maybe we can get him revived at the hospital.'

Oh sure Leah, I thought, people who've been dead a couple of minutes don't revive. And it would take us ages to get him to a hospital.

Still it seemed better to do something than nothing.

I forced myself to go over to Sam's body. All of a sudden it moved slightly and he moaned.

I leaped a mile.

'He made a sound Zak. See he's not dead. We've got to do something to help him,' said Leah.

I moved closer cautiously. I could see his breathing. I went round the other side of him so I could see his face. Sam's eyeballs were moving inside his closed lids.

'Sam, Sam, we're here.'

He slowly lifted his eyelids and looked relieved when he saw me. He moaned again, a deep moan, like in the death scenes in the movies. God, maybe he was still going to die? We did have to do something. There was no colour in Sam's face, and although I had the impression he could see me, he didn't seem able to speak.

I looked at the trap. The spring was pushing it strongly into Sam's leg, but I knew how it worked, from before with the monster. I grabbed the jaws of it and pulled them back. I slid it down off Sam's leg.

It was not a pretty sight. A mashed up ankle and a lot of blood. God it must hurt.

'Help me,' moaned Sam. 'Do something about my leg. It's killing me.'

I felt suddenly really odd - something was happening inside me - something strange - like something was filling me up with fizzing, warm energy.

I heard Laloune say, 'Do you feel the energy coming into your hands Zak?'

I did feel energy in my hands. They were buzzing and alive, full, almost swollen with this warm energy.

'Heal him. You've got to heal him,' said Laloune quietly.

'Heal him? What? How?'

'That's what the energy is for Zak. Reach out and heal Sam with your hands.'

Wow. This was the strangest thing anyone had ever asked me to do. But the way Laloune said it, I didn't wonder any more.

I felt myself go into concentrating mode, like

when I was going to fly but different. Then I filled with even more energy. I looked at Sam's leg where it was damaged with a steady gaze. I thought, deep in my thoughts, of it being unwounded, healthy, OK.

I reached out my hands. It was too revolting to touch, so I just held them as near Sam's leg as I could bear, one on each side.

I looked and looked. I didn't break my gaze or my concentration. I couldn't. The whole thing seemed to be happening to me, beyond my control. It wasn't like something I was planning. It was just happening. As I looked I noticed the blood stop flowing. A scab formed.

'That's it,' said Laloune, 'Keep going like that.'

'What's happening?' asked Leah, 'The wound is disappearing.'

'It's responding to the energy in Zak's hands, and to his mind, which he has emptied of everything except his wish to heal Sam.'

'But that's not possible,' said Leah, 'It was really bad.'

All along the slash where the scab was, we could see the skin was beginning to heal up.

Sam was looking startled, not to say stunned. He had half sat up, propped up on his arm, so that he could see what was going on. He was still a pretty awful colour.

'I must be still asleep,' he muttered. He fell back onto the ground.

'Leah, you help,' said Laloune, 'You work on his head.'

'How?'

'Just put your hands there.'

Leah told me later she hadn't wanted to. But as she moved round to the right place she felt her hands fill up with energy too. Her brother's smelly head was not something she enjoyed touching even if he was in pain. But if Laloune had asked her to do it, she felt she must.

As she put her hands on Sam's head she felt a warm current running between them. Something about the pleasant warmth relaxed her, and Leah began to feel calm.

We sat like that for some time, all three of us in silence, with Laloune looking on. The fierce wind had died down, and the half moon was filling the woods with gentle light. It became very peaceful. The longer we sat, the stiller we got. Sam didn't moan any more. My hands buzzed more gently.

Eventually we all drifted into sleep.

CHAPTER 18

What Happened

I woke first. It was just getting light. Laloune was pulling on my shirt with her beak. 'Zak, come on, it's time to get back to your cabin. The adults will have a fit if the three of you are all absent from your beds when they get up.'

I felt heavy and strange. I knew that something big had happened but it took a moment to reassemble myself and remember where I was.

When I opened my eyes properly and saw Leah and Sam asleep on the ground I came to very quickly. I looked at Sam's leg. It was OK. Quite a lot of dried blood around the ankle, but no gaping wounds, no torn flesh. Perhaps it hadn't been so bad. Perhaps the worst of it had been a dream.

'Leah, Sam, wake up. It's getting light. We've

got to get back inside.'

They both stirred, and woke.

On the way back we stopped at the river's edge to wash Sam's wounds. Underneath all the dried blood we found a large, nasty weal. It was the sort of way skin goes when you've fallen off your bike and ripped the skin off your knee, and weeks later it is all skin covered again, but wrinkly, and never quite as it was before. We all stared at it amazed.

'Was my leg like this last night?' asked Sam.

'Not that I remember,' I said.

'Me neither,' said Leah.

'Have you done this sort of thing before?' asked Sam.

'Never!' I said.

'Me neither,' said Leah.

Sam looked different somehow. 'I feel so strange! Do you want to hear what happened before you found me? You'll never believe it.'

Leah and I looked at each other. Was this Sam talking? Sam who dismissed everything that didn't appear on a screen or have a price tag on it as worthless, useless, and probably not even existing?

'Tell us,' said Leah.

'Yes, tell us,' I said, at the same moment.

'Well, it started like this. I suppose you know I'd found the animal trap in the big house?'

We both nodded.

'Well, last night I decided I would sneak out really late to set my trap. I had to do it late because Mom found out I'd been setting the trap and tried to stop me. Succeeded too, till last night.

'Anyway - I was wandering around looking for a good place. It all looked really different in the dark, and I wasn't too sure where I was. I came across a really thick part of the woods. I reckoned that if I could get my trap in there, I'd be sure to catch something.

'So I squeezed and pushed my way in through some bushes - they were really spiky some of them - and I suddenly felt really, really peculiar. Sort of sick, and dizzy. I felt so bad I wanted to go straight home. But I really wanted to set my trap too. So I crouched down and pulled open the jaws and set the spring. By the time I'd set it I felt even worse. Really sick. I had to lie down right away. I was all woozy and really sleepy. I was as scared as anything to fall asleep in the wood, so I tried to stay awake, but I couldn't.

'I don't know how long I slept, but I had one

of my worst ever nightmares. It was one of my Bing and Bong ones, when they're chasing me, and it goes on and on and won't stop. Only they were so mean looking. Like they really meant to kill me this time. I woke up just as they were about to catch me, and the first thing I saw - and this is the bit you won't believe - was a huge, green monster. He was leaning over me, looking right at me! I mean he was really there - not in my dream, but there, here, in reality! He was much worse than the nightmare. Worse than Terminator, or Frankenstein, or any other monster I've ever seen. Worse because he was real. He was really there. Real. You've no idea how terrifying he was!

'Luckily for me, as soon as I woke up he ran off. I screamed my head off and jumped up in total panic. And put my foot straight into the trap. You can't believe the pain when it closes on your leg. I screamed some more, and then I think I must have fainted, because the next thing I remember is you two being there.

'Then when you started doing that thing with your hands Zak, I was sure that I must still be dreaming after all. It felt so good. How could it feel so good? It was like you were just draining away the pain, and then when Leah came to my head, I began to feel so calm and peaceful and safe. It was really odd. Where on earth did you get the idea to do that if you've never done it before?'

Leah and I looked at each other. Tell Sam about talking with an owl? A few hours ago that would have been out of the question. But now?

I took the risk. 'Laloune the owl told us to.'

'The owl? Is that what it was doing there! But how could it tell you?'

'We both know how to communicate with her.'

Sam flopped backwards on the ground once more. The night had been full of shocks for him. Poor Sam. I felt sorry for him. His reality was breaking open. His world of computer games and shopping malls would never be the same again.

CHAPTER 19

Sam, Leah and Me

After that night Sam, Leah and I became the best of friends. We did everything together.

Leah introduced Sam to her tree house, which he was dead impressed by, and we spent days and days there, taking our supplies from the big house in the morning, hauling them up on the special pulley we made, eating, playing cards, and generally having a great time. Sh'krump often joined us, and although Sam never got the hang of full communication with him, he did get the general gist of it.

We explained to Sam about the nightmare monster, and he was amazed to realize it had come to help him that awful night, even after it got caught in his trap. He felt really terrible about what he had done. He wanted to meet the nightmare monster to apologize, but Sh'krump said no. Sh'krump told us the monster wasn't at ease being with people when they were awake. And anyway it could feel Sam's gratitude as energy, and this was the way it liked to get thanks.

When we told Sam about the zing, and how beautiful it was, and how the nightmare monster needed it to survive, Sam actually cried. He said he'd had no idea the zing was even there. He promised never, never to harm the zing again.

On rainy days, or just for a change, we spent time in my cabin. Sam really liked the trapeze, and we rigged up a new improved landing pad so that we could drop off it in all kinds of ways without crashing.

Laloune enjoyed watching us on the trapeze through the window. She never could get over the fact that humans love so much to almost fly, but mostly haven't learned to fly for real. She was all for Leah learning. Leah did manage to take off a couple of times, but she found it hard to keep her concentration so she crashed pretty quickly. That put her off. I found to my surprise that I couldn't take off at all when I knew Leah and Sam were watching, so I did a lot less flying than usual. But there was plenty else to do.

We played Scrabble and Monopoly and cards. We had midnight feasts, and told ghost stories. We built a go kart with the old pram wheels lying around in the cellar at the big house. We played together on Sam's computer. We played baseball with Anna and a rare appearance from Billy, and swam off the rocks in the best coves that Sh'krump showed us.

When I think of it, I am amazed how much fun it turned out it could be, to be with people. Really, I never did anything much that I enjoyed with other people before. My best companions had been animals. And my Mum and Dad of course. But they're my parents so they don't count. This was entirely the first time I had ever had friends who I could just be completely myself with, who didn't think I was weird, or laugh at me, and who accepted me totally.

So you can imagine I was pretty sad when it was getting to the end of the summer. When one evening Laloune suggested a special meeting with all the animals to say goodbye I said 'No'. I didn't want to say goodbye. Even thinking about it gave me the most horrible feeling. I never felt this feeling before. It was like it was raining and grey and misty inside me. I felt sore and sick and heavy and sad, all mixed up together. It was terrible. I began to wonder if I would survive leaving the island, and my best and only friends.

CHAPTER 20

Writing It Down

Now it was the last week. Everything was very quiet when I got up. The others had all gone shopping, buying presents to take back to people at home. For the first time, I wished I had gone with them.

I ate breakfast, and decided to go for a walk to the clearing.

When I got there, it felt wrong to go into Leah's tree house without her. I stirred the embers from last night's camp fire with a stick. They were still warm and glowing red in the middle.

I sat next to the fire, hoping Sh'krump would appear.

I felt sad and depressed and after half an hour gave up on him and wandered back to my cabin disconsolately.

Once inside I didn't feel like doing anything, not my trapeze, nor my knitting, nor reading. Nothing.

I sat down at the table in the window and stared at the river through the trees. I'd always liked the river so much, but right now it just seemed to separate me from my friends having fun together, eating ice creams and doing their shopping in the town.

I sat like that for a long time.

I picked up a pencil and started doodling. I thought and thought about my time on the island, all the things that had happened and how it was coming to an end. I didn't want it to end. And I didn't want to forget what had happened here - none of it - not one detail, not one day.

Then, out of nowhere, an idea came to me. I could write it all down.

I would write the story of my summer on River Island.

Then I would be able to remember and to make people understand. I could show it to my Dad, I could show it to anyone who hadn't been here. Maybe somebody would understand.

I rooted around in my drawer for paper, and found some unused exercise books. I wrote Ζακ on the cover of one of them, and opened it at the first page.

As you know, since you have already read the first page, I decided that the only place to start was at the beginning - not at the beginning of my time on the island, but at the beginning of my life.

And so you have my story in front of you at this very moment. It's so odd. I mean, here I am sitting here now - not now for you, but now for me, and I am writing this while you are doing something completely different, and now, I mean your now, you, wherever you are, are reading these very words, these words that I am passing through my mind right now, in my now. But they won't be passing through my mind any more when you read this - they will be passing through your mind. That's strange! That's time travel!

After I finished writing the first three chapters, I felt really tired - but good tired, pleased with myself. I'd started! I sat back in my chair and looked at the river again. It seemed beautiful once more, with the light dancing on it, and the boats going by.

I got up and made myself an ice cream soda, and decided to go for a walk before the others got back from the town.

I got the idea to do something I hadn't done yet - to walk all around the island as near as possible to the edge. So instead of setting off on the path towards the clearing, or across to the big house, I turned to the right and went down to the water's edge.

I took off my trainers and paddled. The river lapped around my ankles. Little tiddlers swam in shoals around me. I watched as they all swung into a new direction at the same time. It was warm and nice. I liked it here.

After a while I put on my trainers again, and set off on my intended walk around the island. Much of the way it was easy to keep to the very edge, but in one or two places the trees were too thick or the rocks too tricky to negotiate. I did my best though, because for some reason I wanted to stay as close as possible to the edge of the island. Like I wanted to surround it, all of it.

About half way round I sat down for a rest. From this side of the island the view was different. And you could see the United States. Pretty strange to live somewhere where one way is one country, and the other way is another - to live in the middle of a huge river that separates two huge countries.

I remembered from the map I had studied in London before we came, that the other side of the United States, in the direction I was looking, was the Atlantic Ocean, and then, thousands of miles across the ocean, was England.

I sat there for ages, thinking about returning to London. Maybe it wouldn't be so bad. There was the Planetarium and the number 73 bus. I could take up where I left off with our cat Maxine, and tell the squirrels in the park about Sh'krump. I wondered if they would be able to understand the idea of another country, far away across the water.

And Dad would be there. I hugged my knees up to me as I realised how much I'd missed him. We could play our favourite card games. We could get back to work on our hoverboard invention. Dad was so sure we'd figure out how to make it really fly!

Yes, maybe it wouldn't be too bad.

Maybe I'd go.

I stood up and trotted off around the second half of the island. Just as I was coming back into sight of my cabin, the boat pulled up with everyone on it.

'There's a letter from Dad,' Mum said. 'He's

on his way home. He says hello to everybody
and he promises not to eat all the ice cream
before we get there.'

'How long is it before we see him?'

'A week. We'll be home a week tomorrow, and
he'll be there to meet us. So, it's nearly time to
go back Zak. Are you looking forward to it?'

'Yeah.' I could say this truthfully after my
walk around the island, 'Yeah, I am. But I've still
got a few things to do before we go.'

'What sort of things?'

'Oh, my things, things to help me remember
being here.'

*   *   *

A week. I'd have to get a move on. I made
a plan to spend every morning writing my story.
I wanted to get it done before we left, while I
was still in the atmosphere of being here.

Sometimes at night if I wasn't sleepy I got
up and did a bit more. As you know from
what you've read, I wanted to write a pretty
full account, and then sometimes bits would
creep in that I hadn't expected, that weren't
strictly necessary, but I sort of liked, and wanted
to write anyway. So it wasn't exactly going to

be short.

I was excited about seeing Dad too. I thought of showing him my story, letting him know everything I'd discovered here. Well, maybe not everything, I'd have to think about that.

So the next few days I sat for hours at my table, writing. I filled three exercise books quickly. I was getting there.

Then I got to the terrible night when Sam got his leg caught in the trap. I found I couldn't write this bit by day. It was too intense, and like it was from another reality, and just seemed unbelievable when I wrote by day. So I sat up late into the night to write it. At night things change, and by the time I got to the bit about healing his leg it was after midnight and anything seemed possible.

As you might have guessed, I didn't get much further. I was so exhausted after staying up all night and writing that bit about Sam and the trap, that I slept most of the next day, and then the day after that was the day we left. So you can figure out that as I write these exact words you are reading precisely now (your now I mean, not mine) I'm not sitting on the island. I'm back in my room in London.

I was worried that when I got back here I

would lose the impetus to finish the story, but luckily I have a good reason to finish it because of something that happened a few days before we left - which I'll tell you about now.

*   *   *

One afternoon I was sitting at my table writing. I was beginning to run out of time with only four days to go before we would leave. I was only up to the bit about my first encounter with Leah in her tree house.

I'd done my writing in the morning, and then after lunch started a game of Scrabble with the others. I wasn't getting good scores, and I kept feeling sort of jumpy, so I said I had something I needed to do in my cabin, and went back there. As soon as I came in the door I realised that what I wanted to do was carry on writing. Of course! How stupid of me to even get involved in that game of Scrabble. I had so much to get finished.

I swept some empty crisp packets off my table and sat down. I was in just the right mood to do it, and I got totally absorbed right away. I don't know if you've ever written anything because you wanted to - not something you had to do for school, but something you chose to do - but if you have you probably know what I mean when I say it sort of takes you out of time. You forget everything around you, and exist somewhere different. It's kind of blissful by the way.

Well, I got like that. I don't know how long I'd been there, but all of a sudden somebody giggled right behind me. I nearly jumped out of my skin. It was Leah. She had crept into my cabin without me noticing, and was standing behind me.

'Leah! What on earth are you doing there?'

'Reading,' she said.

'Reading? What are you reading?'

'What you are writing of course.'

'Oh no. You're not reading this are you?' I said covering the page with my arm.

'Yep. Too late to cover it now.'

'You mustn't.'

'Well I have. And anyway, why not? It's interesting. And it's about me.'

I glanced at the page. The last thing it said was *I also knew she could keep a secret better than anyone I'd ever met.*

I felt really embarrassed. My face went all hot.

'Zak you don't have to turn red. It's true. I

149

can keep secrets. You found one of mine. Now I've found one of yours. Does anybody else know you are writing this?'

'No, nobody.'

'Well it's lucky it's me who found you out and not Anna who would immediately tell everyone.'

There was some truth in this. Maybe it wasn't too bad that Leah had seen it. As long as I hadn't said anything rude about her.

'So you thought I was only into girl's things did you?' she laughed. 'And look at all the adventures we've had. Is there any more I can read?'

This was a startling idea. Should I give it to Leah to read?

'Definitely,' said Leah. Drat. I still hadn't got used to Leah's habit of mind reading.

'OK, as long as you promise not to laugh at what I've written or tell anyone. You promise?'

Leah held up her hand solemnly. 'I promise.' I liked Leah. I was going to miss her, badly.

I gave her the first two full exercise books, and she curled up on the old arm chair and started reading. For a while I just sat there, dumbfounded. Then I reckoned I might as well get on with my writing.

. . . I also knew she could keep a secret better

than anyone I'd ever met . . . I was soon right into it again.

When I reached the end of that episode, the bit when Leah gets fed up with me and tells Sh'krump to lead me back home, I pushed my chair back and stretched. Amazing how uncomfortable you can be and not even notice it.

I turned around and there was Leah, asleep on the arm chair, my exercise books on the ground. So she hadn't laughed at me, or if she had I'd been too absorbed in what I was writing to notice.

I was tired too. It had got completely dark outside - it must be pretty late.

I heard Leah's Mum calling her from the big house, 'Leah!'

'Leah, Leah, wake up. Your Mum's calling. You've got to go in.'

'Leah,' her Mum yelled, 'Come in now. It's late.'

Leah got up. She smiled at me sleepily. 'It was great, Zak. I like your story. Will you show me the rest sometime?'

'Yeah, OK, I will. You can read it all. When it's finished.'

'Promise?'

'Promise.'

And so I had to finish it, didn't I, even though now I'm back here in London, with Maxine the cat and the park squirrels for animal company instead of Laloune and Sh'krump, with traffic roaring by outside our house, with street lights making it never dark. Even though it all seems pretty far away and unlikely, I've finished the story of my summer on River Island, and I'm going to send it to Leah in Wisconsin.

P.S.
How I Got my Name

What a coincidence! Two minutes ago, just after I wrote that last bit, I was sitting here feeling all warm inside from having finished my story, and Mum came in with a letter for me from Leah! Of course I read it right away. It's great - apparently she and Sam are getting on better than they ever did before the summer. She's asking me to write down the story of how I got my name. I told Leah on the island, but she says she can't remember all the details and she wants to tell Sam. So I've decided to write it right away. Here goes . . .

People sometimes laugh at me because of my name. It drives me crazy. So what if it rhymes with yak, plaque, mac and whack. It's not what it rhymes with that matters, it's how you got it. That's what I say.

And I know how I got it!

When my Mum was pregnant with me she needed to rest a lot, and she and my Dad got into the habit of playing Scrabble.

One evening they decided to reverse the 'no names' rule and play with only names. They told me afterwards they hadn't thought much yet about what to call me, and this was their way of getting ideas.

I couldn't see the game, as they were playing on the table, but I could hear my Mum muttering under her breath, 'G - R - A - C - E . . . OK . . . Grace.' Grace. What kind of a name is that for a boy? Or did they really have no idea that I was not planning on getting born as a female?

My Dad paused for a while, and then burst out laughing. He put out all his letters across the A of Grace to spell Meatloaf! Mum wasn't too pleased. She told him the idea of playing was to find a name for me. Dad just laughed, 'Well, it is a name isn't it? Got to open up to inspiration Marion!' I didn't think this was funny at all. Meatloaf indeed.

And things weren't getting any better. Mum put Jill and then, on her next turn, John, using the same J. I dreaded her picking another J because these J names didn't sound right to me at all. God preserve me from Jim, Joan, Janet, James, Jackie, Jenny, Jo and Jake. Actually Jake wouldn't have been too bad. (By the way, I've since discovered that there is only one J in Scrabble so I needn't have worried.)

Now Dad was getting frustrated. He wanted to get the right letters for Socrates, but he kept picking I's. He is Greek remember, and his father who he was very fond of, and who has been dead a long time, was called Socrates. Dad seemed to think this was some kind of a reason to call me that. I'd heard him arguing with Mum about this before. I agreed with her. I didn't see why he would want to muddle me up with his father. I would have thought almost the only person in the world you can be absolutely sure isn't your father is your own son.

So next he put Neil on the L of Liam, that he'd put on his last turn, and right away Mum put Nick onto the N. At least they were both laughing now. I guess Mum was relieved that Socrates was so awkward to collect. They were laughing quite a bit.

But I was beginning to get annoyed. I was worried that the fate of my life long name was going to be sealed by the ratio of common and uncommon letters in the Scrabble game, and what's more, was not likely to exceed four letters.

Then my Dad picked a Z.

My Dad can get seriously competitive when he is playing Scrabble, and the sight of this Z made him entirely lose interest in choosing his favourite Greek names and concentrate on getting a high score. (Z, in case you don't already know, is the highest scoring letter in the game.) He let out a yell of delight, and picking up only his A (the one he had been wanting to use for Socrates) and the Z, placed the Z on the triple word score, and the A below it, fitting right onto the K of Nick. 'Forty eight', he said triumphantly. For a minute I thought "Forty Eight" was the name he was suggesting. It wasn't one I'd heard before, but I quite liked the sound of it. Then I heard Mum say 'Zak. . .what a brilliant name! Hey, George, I like that . . . Zak.' She said it like she was tasting it. I liked the way she said it.

'Zak,' said my Dad, as if he hadn't really taken it seriously before. 'Yeah. Zak. Zak . . . Yeah . . . Maybe.'

I, meanwhile was getting very agitated. This Zak name was certainly better than the dreaded

J's, and if I was going to have a short simple name, it had better sound sharp, unusual, and be high scoring. I wanted it, and I wanted them to know I wanted it. I tried my hardest to dig my elbow into my Mum as a signal. She groaned and complained, but didn't seem to make the connection with what was going on. I kept poking her, not knowing what else to do. I didn't want to hurt her, but this was important. I might have this name for a hundred years. I managed to make her uncomfortable enough to suggest they stop the game and go to bed.

Well, that was a major triumph. Now maybe they wouldn't think up any more names. Maybe they would stick with Zak.

And glory be to God, they did!